10. 5.

Mills & Boon Classics

A chance to read and collect some of the best-loved novels
from Mills & Boon—the world's largest publisher of
romantic fiction.

Every month, four titles by favourite Mills & Boon authors
will be re-published in the *Classics* series.

A list of other titles in the *Classics* series can be found
at the end of this book.

Anne Mather

CHASE A GREEN SHADOW

MILLS & BOON LIMITED
LONDON · TORONTO

First published 1973
Australian copyright 1980
Philippine copyright 1980
This edition 1980

© Anne Mather 1973

ISBN 0 263 73328 9

Set in Linotype Baskerville 10 on 12pt

*Made and printed in Great Britain by
Richard Clay (The Chaucer Press), Ltd.,
Bungay, Suffolk*

CHAPTER ONE

TAMSYN STANFORD cupped her chin in her hands and stared moodily through the drug-store window, completely oblivious of the smoky atmosphere and the deafening din of the record machine. Outside a steady drizzle was falling, wetting the sidewalks and causing homeward-bound shop and office workers to quicken their step. Cars swished through puddles, queues formed at bus-stops, but Tamsyn seemed lost in a depressed world of her own making.

Her companion, a rather long-haired young man of her own age, with a drooping moustache, studied her expression thoughtfully, and then said: 'Let me get this straight. Your mother has decided to marry this professor guy she's known for several years?'

'That's right,' answered Tamsyn, nodding, without looking at him. 'He's a sort of friend of the family. He knows my father, too.'

'And during the summer vac they're going on this lecture tour of the west coast as a sort of honeymoon, right?'

'Yes.' Tamsyn sounded impatient. 'I've told you so.'

'I know it. But what I can't understand is—why should you have to change your plans—*our* plans, in fact?'

Tamsyn turned green eyes in his direction. 'Apparently, no matter how she's felt about Daddy in the past, she feels I would be—well, less of an anxiety if I go and spend several weeks with him.'

The young man gave an angry exclamation. 'But,

gee, Tammy, it's crazy! You're almost eighteen. Surely you're old enough to look after yourself! Besides, your father is the last person I'd have expected her to ask you to stay with.'

'It's not a question of looking after me!' Tamsyn was stung to retort. 'And don't call me *Tammy*!'

'Well, it's stupid!'

'I know that.' Tamsyn heaved a sigh. 'But you see, it's not as straightforward as it sounds. When Daddy—well, when they split up, naturally I stayed with Mummy. But later, after the divorce, he was given authority to visit me and have me visit with him. But although he has come very occasionally, Boston isn't exactly on his doorstep, is it?'

'I agree. But similarly Wales isn't on your doorstep either.'

'No. And whenever he has suggested me visiting with him and Joanna Mummy hasn't been very keen. But now—well, she thinks it's the ideal opportunity!' She bent her head. 'I'm sorry, Gerry, but what can I do?'

Gerry Thorpe stubbed out the cigarette he had been smoking with savage movements. 'I think your mother is a selfish——' He bit off an epithet. 'Can't you see what she's doing, Tammy—Tamsyn? I mean, it's obvious that until now she's guarded you jealously, not even allowing you to spend any time with your father. But suddenly, because she wants something, she's prepared to send you to England without a second thought——'

'Not to England, to Wales,' contradicted Tamsyn shortly. 'Oh, what's the use of talking about it? We can't do anything. I shall have to go. We'll just have to cancel our plans, that's all.'

6

'You could defy her.'

Tamsyn shook her head. 'No, I couldn't do that. Look, do you honestly think I'm looking forward to going to—to Trefallath? I can assure you I'm not. I've only met Joanna once and we didn't exactly take to one another, which is only natural, I suppose.'

'The other woman,' remarked Gerry dryly.

'Yes.' Tamsyn lifted her untouched cup of coffee and sipped it experimentally.

'Have you ever been to Wales before?'

'No.' Tamsyn frowned. 'I can hardly remember London, let alone anywhere else. I was only seven when they split up, you know, and Mummy came back to the States.'

'Your father must be like a complete stranger to you.'

'He is. Although on the rare occasions he's visited Boston he's tried to be kind. It's rather a difficult situation for me. I can appreciate the difficulties on both sides. Not that I sympathise with what my father did, of course,' she added hastily. 'He made my mother terribly unhappy.'

'Did he?' Gerry hunched his shoulders sceptically. 'Knowing your mother as I do I can't somehow see her ever being at a loss.'

'That's not a very nice thing to say,' exclaimed Tamsyn indignantly. 'When has she ever been other than polite to you?'

Gerry shook his head. 'Okay, okay, don't bite my head off. I'm just feeling a bit fed up, that's all.'

Tamsyn's face softened. 'I'm sorry, Gerry, truly I am. But I've got to go to Wales. Perhaps we could arrange something for the Christmas vac.'

'Who wants to go hitching in the middle of winter?'

7

asked Gerry gloomily. 'Besides, by then your mother will be good and married to this guy, and who knows, he may decide to move to the west coast if this trip appeals to him.'

Tamsyn's dark brows drew together. 'You don't think he'd do that, do you?'

'How should I know?' retorted Gerry shortly. 'Gee, what a day!' He indicated the rain outside. 'And I was going to suggest we went to the ball game tonight.'

Tamsyn smiled and her companion wondered, with a pang, however Lance Stanford would bear to let her go once she had spent some time with him. In his eyes, Tamsyn was perfect, his ideal, and not the teenage crush his mother thought she was. Tall and slender, yet warmly rounded, Tamsyn was as tall as he was, with straight corn-coloured hair that fell several inches below her shoulders. He had seldom seen her in anything other than jeans and sweaters, and the kind of loose smocks that were so popular nowadays. Yet for all that she retained a certain femininity that attracted her fellow students without any effort on her part. She was a popular girl at college, but she would be the first to admit that boys figured more largely among her friends than girls.

Now she slid off her seat, brushing back her hair with a careless hand. 'I must go,' she said. 'I promised Mummy I'd be home early. Charles is coming to dinner.'

'Charles Penman, I suppose.'

'Correct.' Tamsyn slid the hood of her coat over her head. 'Will I see you tomorrow?'

'I guess so,' conceded Gerry, sighing. 'Aw, heck, Tamsyn, won't you change your mind?'

'I can't, Gerry.' Tamsyn was firm. 'Goodbye.'

''Bye, Tamsyn.' Gerry gave her a swift kiss on the mouth, but before he could prevent her she had slipped away, a hand raised in farewell.

About half an hour later, Tamsyn let herself into her home in Vestry Square. It was one of those tall, narrow old Boston houses which had been successfully modernised and was now a fitting background for Laura Stanford, Tamsyn's mother. Softly textured carpets ran into all the corners, while the elegant staircase which mounted out of the entrance hall was panelled in mellow oak.

Rebecca, Laura's housekeeper and personal maid, encountered her employer's daughter in the hall and gave her slow Southern smile. 'You're back early,' she said in her drawling voice. 'Your mother's not home yet.'

Tamsyn slipped off her coat. 'Mr. Penman's coming to dinner, so I thought I'd give myself plenty of time to bathe and change.' She sighed and looked thoughtfully at Rebecca's shiny black face. 'I suppose you've heard that I'm to stay with Daddy while Mummy and Charles are away.'

Rebecca nodded. 'Yes, Miss Tamsyn. Your mother told me this morning.' She frowned, tipping her head on one side. 'Why? Don't you want to go?'

'No.' Tamsyn tugged impatiently at a strand of hair. 'Well, after all, it's more than three years since I've seen him and then only when he visited Mummy here. I hardly know him.'

Rebecca folded her arms across her ample stomach. 'Then perhaps it's time you did,' she said, with the familiarity of an old servant. 'My, visiting England and all! You'll likely have a wonderful time.'

'My father lives in Wales,' remarked Tamsyn distinctly, walking through into the comfortable lounge that overlooked the quiet square. 'And I'm sure I shan't enjoy it at all. Good heavens, I've scarcely exchanged more than two words with Joanna—she's his second wife, you know.'

Rebecca had followed her and was standing squarely in the doorway. 'It will do you good to get away,' she insisted. 'Besides, you know your mother never approved of you planning that holiday with Gerald Thorpe.'

'I know that.' Tamsyn flung herself moodily into an armchair. 'Why do I have to go away, though? I could perfectly well stay here with you!'

'I shan't be here. I'm to visit my sister in New Orleans.'

Tamsyn pressed her lips together mutinously. 'Then I could stay here alone.'

Rebecca was scandalised. 'Now don't you go upsetting your mother with talk like that. She's only thinking of what's best for you. Why, if I was to be offered a trip like that, I'd be thrilled!'

'Would you, Rebecca?' Tamsyn was doubtful. 'I wonder. I just can't see myself fitting in with them. My father's a doctor, as you know, with a country practice. I've always lived in the city—mixing with eggheads like Mummy and Charles—not nature-lovers!'

'Miss Tamsyn!' Rebecca couldn't hide her impatience. 'Don't you talk like that no more. Your mother's going to be home soon, and how do you think she'd feel if she thought you were so opposed to going to England?'

'Wales,' said Tamsyn automatically, getting to her feet. 'I think I'll take my bath. Oh, don't look so anxious, Rebecca. I shan't say anything to spoil the idyll. I just wish sometimes I was consulted before plans were made for me.'

She was in the bath, her body concealed beneath scented soap bubbles, when her mother entered the bathroom. Laura Stanford was not much like her daughter. Although they were of a similar height and build, Laura's hair was brown and undistinguished, and now she wore it dragged into a rather severe knot which added years to her age. She wore horn-rimmed spectacles, too, and looked every inch the university lecturer she was. Tamsyn had sometimes wondered whether it was her mother's lack of femininity which had driven her father into the arms of a woman who hadn't an original thought in her head. She couldn't really understand how they had ever got married at all. They were not alike. Her mother was so much that breed of American woman who needed to feel intellectually superior to her mate and her father had obviously disliked the image. But such thoughts were faintly traitorous, Tamsyn had decided long ago, and she usually kept them at bay. However, this evening, with the prospect of spending several weeks with her father and his wife uppermost in her mind, she couldn't help the inevitable comparison.

Laura was carrying a sheaf of papers and waved them in her daughter's face playfully. 'Look,' she said. 'I've got your tickets and travelling arrangements.'

Tamsyn smoothed soap over her arms. 'When do I leave?'

Laura appeared not to notice the slightly dry note in Tamsyn's voice and pretended to consult the documents. 'Early on Sunday morning, darling.' She looked at her daughter again. 'Charles thought you would prefer to stay overnight Saturday at the hotel and

11

make a fresh start Sunday morning.'

'I see.' Tamsyn played with a handful of bubbles. 'And you leave Saturday night.'

'That's right, darling. On the first stage of our journey. It's rather exciting, isn't it?'

'If you say so.' Tamsyn couldn't entirely hide her own feelings then.

Laura frowned. 'What's wrong? You're not still hankering over those plans you made with Gerry, are you?'

Tamsyn sighed. 'I saw him this afternoon. He was pretty disappointed, and so am I.'

'But, Tamsyn, even had I not been about to take one of the most serious steps a woman can take, I should still have found the idea of you hitching about the country in the company of that young man rather hard to swallow.'

'Why?'

'Oh, Tamsyn, don't be naïve! You know perfectly well what I mean.'

'Do you think if Gerry and I wanted to do something wrong we'd need to arrange a holiday first?' exclaimed Tamsyn scornfully. 'Honestly, Mummy, it's ridiculous!'

'Very well. Perhaps it is. Perhaps I'm doing you both an injustice. And no doubt in other circumstances I would have to agree. But right now I'm just relieved that you're going to stay with Lance. Besides, it will do you good to travel. And England is a beautiful country, no matter what it's climate's like.'

Tamsyn expelled her breath loudly. 'Okay, Mummy. I won't make a fuss.' She forced herself to be interested. 'Where did you say Charles was lecturing first?'

Laura regarded her intently for a moment as though

realising for the first time that Tamsyn had a mind and a will of her own. Then she shrugged, as though to dispel the unease she had suddenly experienced, and began to tell her daughter the details of their schedule.

Charles arrived before Tamsyn went down to dinner, and when she entered the exquisitely appointed lounge he was standing helping himself to a drink from the cabinet. It was strange, she thought with a pang, that when she returned from visiting her father, Charles would be a permanent fixture here, sharing their lives, and sleeping in her mother's bedroom. She would no longer be able to go into her mother's room in the early hours of the morning and tell her all about the party she had just been to, or climb into bed with her on Sunday mornings and have Rebecca bring them breakfast together.

Charles turned when he heard her step and regarded her admiringly. He was a man in his early fifties, of medium build with a rather angular face and body. Like her mother he, too, lectured at the university, and it was their mutual interests which had brought them together. Tamsyn neither liked nor disliked him, but she could understand his appeal for her mother. Theirs was a blending of minds rather than spirits, but Tamsyn knew that that kind of a union would never do for her.

'You're looking charming, my dear,' he said now, pouring her some sherry with the familiarity of long use. 'Here you are.'

'Thank you.' Tamsyn took the glass and looked down into its depths without drinking the liquid. 'Has it stopped raining yet?'

Charles finished his bourbon and poured himself a second. 'More or less. It's quite cool for June, don't you think?'

Tamsyn nodded, and seated herself comfortably in an armchair, smoothing the skirt of her long amber-coloured caftan about her. 'Mummy tells me you're visiting Seattle first.'

'Yes. Then we'll drive south through California, finishing up at San Diego.'

'A wonderful trip,' commented Tamsyn.

'Indeed.' Charles looked rather smug. 'I'm sure your mother will enjoy it.'

'I'm sure she will,' agreed Tamsyn amicably.

'You're not bitter, are you, Tamsyn?'

'Bitter?' Tamsyn was taken aback. 'No. Why should I be bitter?'

'About being sent to your father, of course. I mean —well, Laura has cared for you all these years without a break, you know. It's time he fulfilled his commitment.'

Tamsyn was staggered. Was that what her mother had said? Had she told Charles that Lance Stanford had virtually disregarded his responsibilities? Tamsyn found this possibility vaguely distasteful. After all, her mother had never encouraged her father to keep in touch with his daughter, and Tamsyn recognised the fact that Lance Stanford must have resented this from time to time. But Tamsyn had always allied herself with her mother, never ever imagining that Laura would take it upon herself to get married again.

But just then Laura came into the room, mature and slightly intimidating in a gown of black silk. 'Oh, good,' she said, when she saw the glass of bourbon in Charles's hand. 'You've helped yourself. I hoped you would.' She allowed him to kiss her cheek. 'After all, you've got to get used to making yourself at home here,

14

hasn't he, Tamsyn?'

Tamsyn managed a faint smile, and then her mother's voice changed: 'Tamsyn, go and find Rebecca, darling. Ask her how long dinner will be. I'm starving.'

Tamsyn got up and went obediently out of the room, closing the door behind her. She understood her mother's request for what it was, an attempt to get her out of the way for a few minutes, but it was not a pleasing experience being made to feel an intruder in one's own home. Perhaps it was a good thing they were going away. By the time they came back the newness of their relationship would have been blunted and perhaps then it would not be so hard to take.

The Boeing 747 landed at London Airport in the early evening, London time. It had not been an arduous journey for Tamsyn, but the time change would take some getting used to. Dinner had been served on the flight, but she had been too strung up to eat anything, the events of the past forty-eight hours gradually taking their toll of her.

Her mother and Charles Penman had been married the previous afternoon in a civil ceremony that had lasted only a few minutes. There had been few guests, mainly members of the university fraternity, and it had all seemed rather cold and irreligious to Tamsyn. But her mother was happy, and that was all that mattered. Laura's happiness was evident in her heightened colour, in the excitement of her voice, and in the way she behaved with an increased confidence.

After the ceremony there had been a private reception before they all left for the airport, Laura and Charles on the first stage of their journey to Seattle, and Tamsyn to stay overnight at the airport hotel to be ready for her flight the next morning.

After her mother had left, Tamsyn had sought the privacy of her room and indulged herself in a way she had not done since she was a child. But the tears had relieved her tension somewhat, and only now, with the huge jet taxiing to a halt outside the airport buildings, did a little of that tension return.

Her father was to meet her at the airport, and she wondered whether Joanna would be with him. She hoped not. She would like to have a few moments alone with her father before coming into contact with her—*stepmother*! It sounded unreal somehow: step-mother. How could one have a stepmother when one's own mother was alive and well? It didn't seem right somehow.

Her cases were cleared without incident and a porter carried them through to the reception lounge. But there was no sign of her father, and her heart sank. Surely he hadn't forgotten she was coming. Surely he hadn't mistaken the time of the flight. Knowing her mother as she did she felt sure all the details would have been arranged meticulously.

She sighed and glanced down at herself. Did she look all right? What would he think of her? She had been a child when last he saw her. Her mother hadn't wanted her to travel in trousers, but in this Tamsyn had been firm. She preferred casual clothes, and besides, the dull green suede trouser suit had cost her mother over two hundred dollars and nothing so expensive could look all bad.

A breeze blew in through an open doorway, taking several strands of her hair and stroking them across her face. She was wiping the hair from her mouth when

16

she became aware that she was being scrutinised rather closely by a man across the lounge from her.

An unaccustomed feeling of apprehension slid down her spine as for a brief moment her gaze locked with his and then she looked away, aware of a strange sense of disturbance. She had never before exchanged such a glance with a man of his age—he could be anything from thirty-five to forty-five—and she felt shaken for a moment. Not that he interested her, she told herself sharply. He was too big, too broad, too muscular, too masculine in every way, with dark skin and dark hair and sideburns that reached his jawline. He was not a handsome man by any standards, although she thought that some women might find his harshly carved features and deeply set eyes attractive; if one found such primitive strength appealing, of course.

She ventured another look at him and found to her embarrassment that he was still watching her, his expression vaguely speculative. Tamsyn turned her back on him, but she was intensely aware of his eyes boring into her shoulder blades and she wished desperately that her father would appear and rescue her from this awful situation.

When a low, deep, faintly musical voice spoke just behind her she almost jumped out of her skin. 'As everyone else appears to have departed, you must be Tamsyn Stanford—are you?'

Tamsyn spun round and to her astonishment she found herself confronted by the man who had been staring at her for the last few minutes. 'I—I—yes,' she stammered. 'I'm Tamsyn Stanford. But—but who are you?'

The man's dark eyes were enigmatic. 'My name is Hywel Benedict. I'm a friend of your father's. As he couldn't come to meet you himself, he asked me to do so.'

'Oh!' Tamsyn was at a loss. 'I—I see.'

The man looked down at her two cases. 'Is this all your luggage?' He bent to lift them easily.

'I—yes—but how do I know you are who you say you are?' She flushed in embarrassment as his eyes narrowed. 'I mean—I've never heard your name before.'

Hywel Benedict considered her pink face for a moment and then he frowned. 'I suppose it never occurred to your father to imagine that a girl from your background should consider there was anything sinister about my meeting you instead of him.'

'What do you mean—my background?' Tamsyn was stung by his tone.

'Why, nothing,' he responded expressionlessly. He stood down her cases again and put his hand inside the jacket of his casual sports suit and brought out a wallet. He extracted a photograph and handed it to her silently and Tamsyn tried to concentrate on the images imprinted upon it with some degree of composure. She recognised her father at once, and the small dark woman who she guessed was Joanna, although it wasn't a very good likeness. And standing slightly behind them two other people; a woman, and the definite likeness of the man at her side.

'Thank you,' she said stiffly, handing him back the photograph and feeling rather foolish. 'Yes, this is all my luggage. Do we go?'

'We go,' he agreed, and strode away across the hall without waiting to see whether she was following him.

Outside it was a perfect summer evening, only a faint breeze to cool the warm atmosphere. Hywel Benedict slung her cases into the back of a rather shabby-looking station wagon and then opening the passenger side door indicated that Tamsyn should get in.

Tamsyn did so not without some reluctance. This was not the welcome she had expected to get and she was feeling decidedly tearful. Why hadn't her father come to meet her, or even Joanna if he wasn't able? Instead of this abrupt stranger who seemed prepared to think the worst of her without even waiting until he knew her.

The man climbed in beside her, his thigh brushing hers as he did so. He was such a big man, he succeeded in making Tamsyn, who had always found herself on eye-level terms with the young men of her acquaintance, feel quite small. He smelt of tweeds and tobacco, shaving soap and a clean male smell that made Tamsyn's nostrils twitch a little. She wondered who he was, and what he did, and where he lived, and then chided herself for being curious about a man who was so obviously far out of her sphere of experience. He was her father's contemporary, after all, not hers.

The station wagon responded smoothly beneath his strong-fingered hands, and he negotiated the airport traffic with only slight impatience. For a moment, Tamsyn was diverted by driving on the left-hand side of the road, and then she ventured another look at her companion.

Where his wrists left the white cuffs of his shirt she could see a thick covering of dark hair, while a gold watch glinted against his dark skin. He wore only one ring and that was on the third finger of his left hand, a gold signet ring engraved with his initials.

As though becoming aware of her scrutiny he glanced her way at that moment and encountered her startled green eyes. 'Did you have a good trip?'

19

Tamsyn took an uneven breath. 'It was all right, I suppose. I've not travelled a lot, so I wouldn't really know.' She sighed. 'Where is my father? Why couldn't he meet me?'

'He's at home—in the valley.'

'*At home*?' Tamsyn sounded indignant.

'That's right. Your father's a doctor, Tamsyn Stanford. Doctors here cannot simply leave their work without good reason.'

'And meeting me wasn't a good reason,' observed Tamsyn shortly.

'It wasn't absolutely necessary in the circumstances,' conceded Hywel Benedict. 'I had to come to London anyway, so I offered to meet you.'

'I see.' Tamsyn swallowed the retort that sprang to her lips. 'How is he?'

'Lance? Oh, he's all right.' He spoke with a faint accent which she couldn't identify but reluctantly found attractive. His whole speaking voice was attractive and she had to force herself to think of other things. But he was the most disturbing man she had ever met.

'Are you a doctor, too, Mr. Benedict?'

Hywel Benedict shook his head. 'No. Healing men's bodies is not for me.'

Tamsyn frowned. It was a strange reply to make and she was curious to know exactly what he did do, but she didn't like to ask. Looking out on to countryside that was amazingly like the New England countryside back home, she asked: 'Where are we?'

'Approaching Maidenhead. Our destination, as you know, is Trefallath, but we have some distance to travel before we cross the border.'

'The border.' Tamsyn was intrigued. 'The border

between England and Wales, of course.'

'Of course. Though it's no border as you know it. Merely a continuation of the road.' His tone was dry, and she detected it.

'Are you a nationalist, Mr. Benedict?'

'A nationalist?' A slight smile lightened his dark features. 'And what would you know of such things, Tamsyn Stanford?'

'I read books,' retorted Tamsyn shortly. 'I've read about the Welsh people. I know of their language, and the way they're trying to retain their individuality.'

'Do you now?' His mocking voice disturbed her. 'And why would an American girl like yourself be interested in us poor barbarians?'

Tamsyn flushed. 'You forget, Mr. Benedict. I'm half Welsh myself.'

'Ah, yes, I had forgotten. But perhaps I can be forgiven for so doing. A hybrid like yourself, reared in the artificial atmosphere of the hothouse, is hardly likely to display the characteristics of its less cultivated ancestry, is she?'

'I think you're being offensive, Mr. Benedict,' said Tamsyn, unreasonably hurt by his words.

'Offensive, is it?' His low attractive voice mocked her. 'And why would you think that?'

'I get the feeling that you consider me lacking in some way,' replied Tamsyn evenly. 'Is it because this is the first time I've come to stay with my father?'

Hywel Benedict stood on his brakes as a vehicle overtook them and then cut in dangerously closely in front of them. 'Well, you haven't exactly taken a deal of interest in his affairs before now, have you?'

'There were reasons.'

'I know it. Your mother.'

'Is that so unreasonable?'

'Possessive woman, your mother,' he commented dryly. 'Until it became necessary to shift the responsibility for a period.'

Tamsyn gave him an angry stare. 'I don't require anyone to take responsibility for me. I'm quite capable of taking care of myself. If my father hadn't wanted me here, he could always have refused——'

'Now hold it, Tamsyn Stanford. I never said that your father didn't want you here, did I? On the contrary, I should imagine he is waiting in anticipation for you to arrive. My comments are my own.'

'Then perhaps you should keep your comments to yourself,' retorted Tamsyn, staring with concentration at the passing landscape in an effort to rid herself of the feeling that this man had aroused within her. A feeling of unease, and inadequacy, that did not make her feel good.

They drove on for some distance in silence, while Tamsyn endeavoured to take an interest in her surroundings. The countryside around them was gently undulating, green fields stretching away on either side, interspersed with woodland and winding streams. They passed through places with unfamiliar names like Nettlebed and Shillingford and Abingdon, and Tamsyn caught tantalising glimpses of old churches that in other circumstances she would have liked to have had identified. Had her father met her, as she had expected him to do, it would have been different, and she tried to quell a feeling of indignation which was likely to colour her judgement when she did meet him again.

Hywel Benedict seemed perfectly content to drive in silence, occasionally taking out a pipe and putting it in the corner of his mouth and lighting it absently, only to put it out again after a few inhalations. Tamsyn was tempted to say she objected to the strong aroma it emitted, but as it wouldn't have been entirely true, she said nothing.

At last, she broke the silence by saying: 'Do you live at Trefallath, Mr. Benedict?'

'I live in the valley,' he conceded slowly. 'Trefallath you will find is little more than a cluster of houses. The real population of the valley is spread out among the farms in the area. But no doubt you'll discover all this for yourself.'

Tamsyn sighed. 'It sounds remote. My mother said it was once.'

'Did she now?' Hywel Benedict inclined his head. 'She's right, of course. It is remote. But we like it that way.'

Tamsyn shook her head. 'But what do you do for entertainment?' She coloured. 'I mean, don't you have any desire to be nearer London—or Cardiff, if that is the right place? Don't you feel—well, out of touch?'

Hywel Benedict looked at her out of the corners of his eyes. 'Out of touch with what? What do your cities have to offer us?'

Tamsyn gave an impatient exclamation. 'Surely it's obvious! The cultural assets one finds there! The exhibitions; theatres; concerts! Don't you care for books, or films, or music?'

He shook his head slowly. 'Of course we care for these things. But do you honestly suppose that they're confined to your cities? There's more life in the valley than ever you will find in Cardiff, or London, or Boston either, for that matter.'

Tamsyn was irritated by the way he spoke, as

though he was explaining the facts of life to a recalcitrant child. What could he know about it if he had lived in Trefallath all his life? He was merely using his age and experience against her youth and immaturity. But academically speaking she should be able to annihilate him.

'I don't think we're talking about the same things,' she remarked, in a voice that was intended to sound cool and patronising.

'I think we are,' he contradicted her insistently. 'You think because you've lived in a city all your life that you've become worldly, that you are necessarily more cultured'—the way he said the word was a mockery—'that you are better educated, infinitely more intelligent; not so!' He shook his head again. 'You're just a little girl copying the mannerisms of her elders!' He gave a slight smile. 'I guarantee you'll learn more about life and incidentally about yourself in these few weeks in the valley than ever you learned in that cultivated cabbage patch you call home.'

Tamsyn took a deep breath. 'You don't like me at all, do you, Mr. Benedict?'

Hywel Benedict moved his broad shoulders lazily. 'Now don't be silly, Tamsyn Stanford. I don't know you well enough yet to decide whether or not I like you. But young people today tend to imagine that they understand things a whole lot better than my generation did twenty years ago, and I find it all rather monotonous. I don't know what that mother of yours has taught you, but I think you'd do well to remember that you aren't old enough to act the sophisticated woman of the world even with an uncultured savage like myself.'

Tamsyn was taken aback. 'At least in my country we

treat young people as individuals with original ideas of their own!' she replied heatedly.

'So it's your country now, is it?' He smiled mockingly. 'We're not concerned with our Welsh ancestry any more, is that it, *bach*?'

Tamsyn pressed her lips together irritably. He was the most infuriating man she had ever met and completely outside her range of experience. But where had she gone wrong? What had she said to create this friction between them? She sighed. It was simply that he rubbed her up the wrong way and his calm indifference was somehow hard to take.

'You're deliberately trying to make me say things I'll regret later,' she accused. 'Why? What have you got against me?'

Hywel Benedict's expression hardened for a moment, and she wondered what he was thinking behind those enigmatic black eyes. It was impossible to tell, and when he said: 'Why, nothing, *bach*,' she was almost disappointed.

CHAPTER TWO

CLOUDS were rolling up from the hills ahead of them and Tamsyn shivered, although it was a warm evening. How much farther had they to travel? Would it be dark before they got there? There was something faintly menacing about the prospect of driving in the dark with Hywel Benedict.

Presently, he slowed and she saw ahead of them a small wayside public house. Its timbered façade was rather attractive, and when he turned into the parking area she glanced at him questioningly.

'We'll stop here for something to eat,' he said. 'Are you hungry?'

Tamsyn was tempted to retort that she couldn't eat a thing, but she found she was hungry after all, and there was no point in depriving herself to irritate him, for she felt quite sure he was completely indifferent to her reply.

Nodding her acquiescence, she waited until he stopped the car and then opened her door and climbed out. A faint breeze cooled the air and she watched her companion as he slammed the car door and came round to her side. She eyed her cases on the back seat rather doubtfully, particularly as he had not locked the car, and as though sensing her indecision, he said: 'Would you rather I put them in the boot?'

Tamsyn studied his dark features. 'Will they be safe?'

'Have faith,' he remarked dryly, and walked away towards the lighted entrance.

Grimacing, Tamsyn followed him, and caught him up at the door. She was too interested in her surroundings to argue with him and she wondered in anticipation what they would have to eat. Steaks, perhaps. Or salmon salad. Her mouth watered. It would be her first taste of English cooking for ten years.

A smoky passageway led through to a bar at the back of the building. There were several people in the bar which was discreetly lit and exuded an atmosphere of tobacco and spirits. But where was the food? Tamsyn's stomach gave a hollow little rumble and she glanced up defensively as Hywel Benedict looked down at her in amusement.

'What do you want to drink?' he asked. 'I know you're not eighteen, but no one here does, so how about a shandy?'

'A shandy?' Tamsyn frowned. 'All right.' She wasn't quite sure what he meant. 'But where do we eat?'

'Here.' He indicated the bar stools which lined the attractive little bar, and she slid on to one with some misgivings.

'What do you mean—here?' she whispered as he took the adjoining stool.

'Wait and see,' he advised, summoning the bartender without any apparent effort. 'A shandy and a beer, please.' He looked along the counter and Tamsyn, following his gaze, saw an assortment of bar snacks under perspex covers at the other end. There were meat pies and sandwiches, fruit tarts and cakes, and her heart sank.

'Is this what you mean by something to eat?' she demanded impatiently.

'Yes, why? Did you expect a chic eating house?'

'I thought we'd have a proper meal, yes,' she answered shortly.

'Why, this is a proper meal, *bach*! You wait until you taste those pies. Mouthwatering, they are.'

Tamsyn reserved judgement, but later, after Hywel Benedict had had the barman provide them with a selection of food from which they could take their choice, she had to admit he was right. The meat pies were thick and juicy, and washed down with the mixture of beer and lemonade which her companion had ordered for her they were satisfyingly delicious. There were hard-boiled eggs, too, and a crisp salad that the barman's wife provided, and lots of pickled onions that Tamsyn firmly avoided.

Hywel Benedict ate heartily, talking most of the time to the barman about the state of the weather and the crops and the possibilities of a drought. He swallowed the huge glasses of beer without turning a hair, and Tamsyn, used to seeing her mother's acquaintances tackling small glasses of bourbon or gin, was staggered at his capacity.

Once he caught her eyes on him and held her gaze for a long moment, causing the hot colour to run up her cheeks, and she was reminded once again of that moment in the airport lounge when she had encountered him scrutinising her. She bent her head in embarrassment, conscious of a prickling along her nerves and a quickening beat in her heart. It was crazy, but when he looked at her like that, something tangible semed to leap between them, and she knew that she could never be indifferent to this man, despite the disparity of their ages. She tried to think of Gerry, of his fair-skinned face and gentle brown eyes, and failed abysmally. All she could see were deep-set eyes and

28

darkly engraved features bearing all the unconquered arrogance of his Celtic forebears.

At last, after she had refused a second slice of apple cake, he suggested they should go, and she willingly agreed. She was allowing this man too much space in her thoughts at a time when she should have been thinking of her forthcoming encounter with her father or speculating on what kind of a honeymoon her mother was having.

It was growing dark and a glance at her watch which she had changed to British time when they landed told her that it was nearing ten o'clock. She climbed into the car and when he got in beside her and reached for his pipe, she said:

'How much longer will it be before we reach Tre-fallath?'

Hywel Benedict lit his pipe before answering, and then exhaling smoke, he answered: 'Oh, perhaps another hour and a half—something like that. Why? Getting nervous?'

Tamsyn did not deign to answer that and with a shrug of the heavy shoulders he leaned forward and started the car.

Darkness brought its own uneasiness to a landscape which was fast becoming wilder and less closely popu-lated. The lights of villages were fewer and farther be-tween and Tamsyn gripped her seat tightly, her nerves playing tricks with her. It was all very well contem-plating this visit from the calm and civilised environs of her mother's world, and quite another encountering the stark facts of reality. Here she was, miles from any-thing or anyone she knew or cared about, in the com-pany of a man who had identified himself only by means of a photograph and had since made no attempt to tell her anything about her father or even about himself.

'Relax.'

The calm word startled her into awareness and she stole a look at his shadowy profile. 'Do you know my father very well?' she asked.

Hywel Benedict inclined his head slowly. 'You might say that. We've known each other since we were children together, so I suppose I know him as well as any man could.'

Tamsyn nodded. 'So you'll know—Joanna, too.'

'Joanna is my cousin.'

'Oh!' Tamsyn swallowed this information with difficulty. 'I see.'

'What do you see, I wonder,' he commented wryly. 'Very little beyond that small nose, I shouldn't be surprised.'

Tamsyn unbuttoned and then buttoned the jacket of her suit. 'I don't know what you mean.'

'No? I would have thought a bright little mind like yours would have fastened on to the fact that if Joanna is my cousin she must have known your father a long time, too.'

'Oh, that.'

'Yes, that. It may interest you to know that Joanna was going to marry Lance long before he met Laura Stewart.'

Tamsyn gasped, 'I didn't know that.'

'I don't suppose you did. It's not the sort of thing your mother would have told you, is it? I mean—well, it puts her in a different position, doesn't it?'

'My mother is no *femme fatale*, if that's what you're implying,' stated Tamsyn hotly.

'No. She was never a handsome woman, I'll give you

that,' he remarked annoyingly. 'But she had charm, when she chose to exert it, and I think Lance was flattered.'

'How do you know what she was like?' demanded Tamsyn.

'Because I knew her, too. We were all in London at the same time. I even went to their wedding.'

Tamsyn was stunned. 'I see,' she said, rather uncertainly.

'I didn't approve of Lance marrying your mother,' he continued complacently. 'She wanted Lance to be something he could never be—an intellectual. He didn't belong in London. He pined for the valley. For the simple, uncomplicated life. And eventually he gave up the struggle and went back there.'

'And I suppose you encouraged him,' accused Tamsyn scornfully.

Hywel shook his head slowly. 'Oh, no, *bach*. It was nothing to do with me. I was in South Africa at the time, and I knew nothing about it until I came home and found Joanna and Lance together again.'

Tamsyn compressed her lips. 'And I suppose you approved of that.'

'Naturally. Joanna has made your father happy. Would you rather he had been miserable all his life?'

'How dare you imply that my mother would have been responsible for his own lack of confidence?' Tamsyn was furious.

'Call it familiarity, Tamsyn Stanford. And don't get so angry. You didn't expect to hear good things of your mother in Trefallath, did you?'

'It seems to me that my mother was justified in refusing to allow me to visit with my father before now.'

'Why?' Hywel shook his head. 'There are always two

sides to every question, aren't there? Perhaps if the two had been more evenly balanced, it wouldn't have come as such a shock to hear the other side now.'

'You don't imagine I believe everything you've said, do you?' exclaimed Tamsyn disdainfully.

Hywel made an indifferent gesture. 'No matter. You'll learn, *bach*.'

It was nearly half past eleven when they began the descent into the valley. Tamsyn, who had not expected to feel tired yet, was beginning to sense a certain weariness in her limbs, and her head dropped several times. But she would not allow herself to fall asleep and risk waking to find herself with her head on his shoulder. Somehow she needed to avoid physical contact with Hywel Benedict.

Trefallath was, as Hywel had told her, merely a cluster of cottages, a public house, a school and a chapel. They ran through the dimly lit main street and then turned on to the rough moorland again, following a narrow road which badly needed re-surfacing. At last the station wagon slowed and turned between stone gateposts, and came to a shuddering halt before a low, stone-built house with lights shining from the lower windows.

'Welcome to Glyn Crochan, Tamsyn Stanford,' he remarked, almost kindly, and then slid out of the car.

As Tamsyn got out, light suddenly spilled on to her, and she realised the door of the building had opened and a man had emerged followed closely by the small figure of a woman.

The man greeted Hywel warmly, and then came round the car to Tamsyn with swift determined strides. 'Tamsyn!' he exclaimed, and there was a break in his voice. 'Oh, Tamsyn, it's good to see you!'

32

Tamsyn allowed her father to enfold her in his arms, but she felt nothing except a faint warming to his spontaneous affection. 'Hello, Daddy,' she responded, as he drew back to look into her face. 'It's good to see you, too.'

'My, how you've grown,' went on Lance Stanford in amazement. 'I—I expected a child. It was foolish of me, I know, but I could only think of you that way.' He released her shoulders but took possession of her hand. 'Come! Come and meet Joanna again.'

He drew her firmly after him round the car to where Tamsyn's stepmother waited. Tamsyn had been so intent on appraising her father, noticing how young and lean he looked, how his hair still sprang thickly from his well-shaped head, that she had paid little attention to anything else. But now, as she followed her father round the car, she looked towards the opened door where, in the shaft of light, Joanna Stanford was standing.

And then an almost audible gasp rose to her throat to be checked instantly. Joanna was small and dark and attractive, in a yellow silk dress that moulded her figure in the slight breeze that blew off the moors. She was also most obviously pregnant.

Tamsyn's eyes darted swiftly to Hywel Benedict's and she encountered his sardonic gaze resentfully. He *could* have told her. He could have warned her of what to expect.

And yet that was exactly what he would not do. He would make nothing easier for the daughter of Laura Stewart.

'Joanna darling,' her father was saying now. 'Here she is, at last. Here's Tamsyn! Don't you think she's grown into quite a young lady?'

Joanna smiled and kissed Tamsyn's cheek, welcoming her to Trefallath. In a more receptive mood Tamsyn would have glimpsed the appeal in Joanna's dark eyes, but right now she was too absorbed with her own emotions to make anything more than a desultory response, and avoid making any obvious remarks.

'Come, let's go inside,' said her father, after these preliminary greetings. 'Hywel, you'll come in and have a drink with us?'

'Thank you, no.' Hywel plunged his hands deep into the pockets of his tweed suit. Tamsyn looked at him rather desperately. Now that he was going, now that he had unloaded her cases and placed them on the step for her father to deal with, she was loath that he should go. She scarcely knew her father, after all, and during the past five hours she had come to know Hywel Benedict disturbingly better than that.

'Er—thank you—for bringing me here,' she said unevenly.

Hywel looked down at her mockingly. 'It was a pleasure, *bach*,' he responded.

'Will—will I see you again?' Tamsyn didn't quite know why she should have asked such a question and she was aware that her father was beginning to chafe with impatience to get her inside.

'Without a doubt,' said Hywel, opening the door of the station wagon. 'Your father knows where I live. Goodnight.'

'Goodnight.'

Lance Stanford raised his hand in farewell and the heavy vehicle turned and drove away. Tamsyn glanced back once as Joanna urged her inside, into the warmth and light of the polished hallway, and then gave her attention to her immediate surroundings.

She awoke reluctantly next morning, feeling the rays of the sun as it played upon her eyelids. She rolled on to her stomach, burying her face in the pillows, not wanting to remember where she was, or think of the prospect of the days and weeks ahead of her.

Her room was small but compact, with a single, spring-interior divan and oak furniture. Used to fitted carpets, Tamsyn had found the linoleum-covered floor rather chilling to her feet, but there was a soft rug beside her bed where she had undressed the night before.

The night before...

She sighed. She had not made a good impression and she knew it. She thought perhaps her father had been disappointed in her attitude, but she couldn't be sure. Her own feelings were easier to assimilate. She had found her father the same gentle man he had always seemed to her, but she felt no real emotion towards him. And Joanna it was difficult to see in any other light than that of the woman who had broken up her parents' marriage. It might be true that Laura had not been the ideal wife for a man like Lance, but nevertheless, that didn't alter the fact that it had been her father who had left her mother, not the other way around. She had expected it to be difficult, coming here, but not half as difficult as it was going to be now that she had found that Joanna was pregnant.

She ought not to be shocked, she had told herself over and over again, but she was. And why? Her father was still a young man, after all, barely forty, and it was only natural that he and Joanna should want children. But if only they had not chosen this particular time when Tamsyn had to be there, to see it. She had made no comment about Joanna's condition the night

35

before, and nor had they. But sooner or later she would have to, and she dreaded it. She didn't know much about pregnancies, but judging by Joanna's size it could surely not be much longer before she had the child. And where would she have it? In hospital? It seemed unlikely when her father was a doctor. So she would have it here, quite possibly while Tamsyn was staying.

Tamsyn slid abruptly out of bed. Such thoughts were not conducive to a peaceful frame of mind at this hour of the day and she determinedly walked to the window and looked out on the scene that spread out before her.

The landscape was green and rolling, and somewhere she could hear the sound of running water. But what amazed her most was its emptiness, acres and acres of rolling moorland without a house or village spire to be seen. Away to the left, in a fold of the hills, she knew the village of Trefallath nestled, but here there was nothing but the tree-strewn marches populated by sheep and goats and the lonely cry of the curlew.

She drew away from the window and glanced at her watch. It was a little after eight, and she wondered what she should do. Go downstairs, she supposed. After all, she could hardly expect Joanna to run after her, and nor did she want her to. But she wondered where her father was. Where did he have his surgery? Surely not here, some distance from the village. How on earth did Joanna stand the loneliness?

She washed in the bathroom with its disturbingly noisy geyser gurgling away beside her and then dressed in jeans and a sleeveless sweater. She didn't bother with make-up, but combed her thick hair into some kind of order before leaving her room.

As she descended the staircase she could hear Joanna singing in the kitchen, and she sighed. There was no point in maintaining a kind of armed truce with someone with whom one was going to have to spend a great deal of time, she decided reasonably, with a pang of remorse for her mother. But her mother was not here, she was, and nothing she said would alter the inevitable. With determined brightness, she turned the handle of the kitchen door and entered the room.

Joanna was at the stove, her face shiny from the heat of the pans. 'Oh, good morning,' she said, in surprise. 'You're up, then! I was going to bring your breakfast up to you.'

Tamsyn bit her lip. 'There's no need for that, really. I'm perfectly capable of getting up and making my own breakfast. Besides, in—in your condition, you should be resting, shouldn't you?'

Joanna stopped what she was doing and looked squarely at her stepdaughter. 'You noticed, then.'

Tamsyn coloured. 'Yes. Where's my father?'

'He's gone to see Mrs. Evans. She had a seizure in the night.' Joanna frowned. 'You didn't say anything to your father last night.'

'No.' Tamsyn moved her shoulders defensively. 'Look, Joanna, I'll be honest with you. I didn't want to come here, but my mother wanted me to, so I came.' She sighed. 'Last night I was tired. It was quite an ordeal coming here—alone. I—well, needed time to think.'

'And now you've thought,' said Joanna.

'Yes.'

'You didn't think that your father might be hurt by your not mentioning it sooner?'

37

Tamsyn moved her head. 'Look—it's difficult for me, too, Joanna.'

'And from your expression last night it wasn't just difficult, it was unacceptable, wasn't it?'

Tamsyn scuffed her toe, her hands tucked into the belt of her jeans. 'I guess so.'

'Why? What's so unacceptable about two married people loving one another enough to want children? Wasn't that what your mother and father did when they had you?'

'That was different!' Tamsyn felt uncomfortable. 'Well, no, I guess it wasn't. But just give me time. I— I'll get over it.'

'And in the meantime your father has to worry about you, eh?' Joanna turned back to the stove.

'It's not like that,' exclaimed Tamsyn indignantly. 'Good heavens, he surely didn't expect me to behave as though everything was as it should be! I mean—I scarcely know him! Let alone feel at home with him!'

'Whose fault is that?'

'Why, no one's, I guess.'

'You blame your father for everything, don't you?' Joanna ladled scrambled eggs on to a plate.

'No—that is—no, I don't.' But she did, and Joanna knew it. 'Look—can't we start again? I know it's difficult for you, too. But if I'm to stay here, we can't go on like this.'

'I agree.' Joanna came to the scrubbed wooden table that dominated the kitchen. She rested her hands on the table and looked into Tamsyn's flushed young face. 'All right, Tamsyn, We'll begin again. I won't make things difficult for you, if you don't make things difficult for me.'

'What do you mean?' Tamsyn frowned.

38

Joanna shook her head. 'You really don't know your father very well, do you? Do you honestly think that your attitude last night didn't upset him? Don't you realise that he thinks the world of you? He always has. He hasn't seen much of you, but maybe that's why he's built you up in his mind into something—something marvellous, terrific! His daughter! His Tamsyn! That side of him hasn't been easy to live with, believe me! And now you're here, and if you think things can go on as before so long as you remain indifferent to him, you're mistaken. You'll always come first in his thoughts, I've known that for years, and after you'd gone to bed last night he was like a bear with a sore head, worrying about your reactions. He knew the sight of me had shocked you, and I think if he could have changed things there and then he would have done. But when we went in for this child we didn't know we were going to have you to stay!'

'Oh, Joanna!' Tamsyn felt terrible. 'I—I didn't know—I didn't realise.'

'How could you? So far as you were concerned your father was the villain of the piece. Well, he isn't, and he never was. But that's another story.'

'I'm sorry.' Tamsyn didn't know what to say.

'That's all right. I just wanted to get things straight between us before your father gets back.' Joanna straightened and turned back to the stove. 'Do you like your bacon crisp or not?'

Tamsyn moved to the table, fingering a fork absently. 'Do you think I could just have toast? I'm not very hungry, actually.'

Joanna clicked her tongue. 'No, I don't think you could just have toast,' she retorted, but there was a faint suggestion of a smile touching the corners of her

39

mouth. 'And there's no point in moping about what's been said. You're seventeen, Tamsyn, nearly eighteen, in fact. It's time you grew up. As you said earlier, we've got to live together for the next few weeks, so we might as well make the best of it.'

Tamsyn nodded. 'All right. I'm willing.'

'Good. Then we understand one another.' Joanna flexed her back muscles wearily. 'I shall be glad when these few weeks are over, and I don't mean because of you. I feel so big and clumsy, particularly now, in comparison to you.'

Tamsyn glanced down self-consciously. 'Don't be silly,' she said. 'You're much smaller than I am. I feel quite tall beside you.'

Joanna smiled. 'I always wanted to be tall and slim like you. You're lucky. You've inherited your height and build from your father. Do you know his hair used to be that colour once?'

'You must tell me about him,' suggested Tamsyn quietly. 'I—I'd like to hear about his life before he—he married my mother.'

'Hywel told you I knew him then, of course.'

Tamsyn felt her nerves tingle at the mention of Hywel Benedict's name. 'Yes,' she said, taking a seat at the scrubbed table and resting her chin on her hands, elbows supported on the wooden surface.

Joanna scooped bacon and eggs on to a plate and put it before her. It smelt marvellous and Tamsyn realised she was hungry after all. There was crusty bread to go with it, and yellow butter that melted on the toast that followed.

Joanna joined her at the table, but she had only some toast and Tamsyn commented upon it. 'I need to lose some weight, actually,' confided her stepmother with a sigh. 'We may not have much to offer here, but at least the food is good and wholesome, and I'm afraid I can't resist hot scones with butter and lots of suety puddings.'

Tamsyn laughed. She was beginning to realise that Joanna was not at all as she had expected her to be, and she blamed herself for presupposing things she really knew nothing about.

'Hywel Benedict is your cousin, isn't he?' she asked Joanna now, unable to resist the question.

'That's right.' Joanna poured more coffee into Tamsyn's cup.

Tamsyn hesitated. 'Does he live far from here?'

Joanna looked at her squarely. 'Not far. Why?'

Tamsyn shrugged with what she hoped was nonchalance. 'I was curious, that's all.'

'You didn't mind Hywel meeting you, did you? I mean, Lance couldn't leave the practice without anyone to cover for him, and I was in no fit state to drive nearly two hundred miles.'

'No. No, of course not.' Tamsyn shook her head. 'I guess I did at first, but then...' She pushed her empty plate aside. 'That was delicious. Thank you.'

'I like cooking,' said Joanna simply. 'And I like to watch people enjoy their food.'

Tamsyn glanced round. 'What can I do to help you?'

'Do you want to help?'

'Yes. I don't intend to spend my days loafing around. That's not my scene.' Tamsyn rose from her seat and carried her dirty plates across to the sink. 'Shall I start with these?'

Joanna rested against the table, half turned towards her. 'If you like.'

Tamsyn nodded and filled the bowl with hot soapy water. Outside the kitchen windows she could see a vegetable garden and beyond, a path leading down through wild rose and gorse bushes to a stream, the stream which she had heard earlier. There were some hens picking about behind the back door and several outbuildings which she supposed were used to house livestock. Plunging her hands into the hot water, looking out on that rural scene, she felt a sudden sense of peace and relaxation and she sighed. Maybe it wasn't going to be so bad after all.

Her father returned as Tamsyn and Joanna were making the beds. He came upstairs to find them and looked in surprise at the two of them, folding sheets beneath the mattress. 'What's going on?' he asked, his gaze going from one to the other of them, and Tamsyn smiled.

'Joanna's been telling me what a terror you were when you were a teenager,' she replied, and saw her father's gaze go swiftly to his wife's.

'That's right,' said Joanna calmly. 'There's no better way of getting to know someone than by working together, don't you agree?'

Lance looked bewildered. 'If you say so.' He bit his lip. 'Well, one of you come and make me some coffee. I'm sorely in need of a stimulant. Mrs. Evans has been at her most trying.'

'The woman with the seizure?' asked Tamsyn.

'Seizure!' muttered her father grimly. 'It was no seizure. Just the result of overeating, that's all.'

Joanna chuckled and then she said: 'You go with your father, Tamsyn. You know where everything is now. You make him some coffee while I finish off here and then I'll join you.'

42

Tamsyn hesitated. 'Are you sure you wouldn't like to make the coffee?'

'Quite sure,' answered Joanna, straightening her back with a firm hand.

Downstairs, Lance faced his daughter rather doubtfully, and Tamsyn considered for a moment, and then said: 'It's going to be all right, Daddy.'

Her father stared at her anxiously. 'What do you mean?'

'I mean my being here—Joanna and me! It's going to be all right. We—we understand one another now.' She sighed. 'And I'm sorry I was so anti-social last night.'

Lance twisted his lips. 'It was understandable, I suppose.'

'You mean—because Joanna's pregnant?'

'Yes.' Her father turned away. 'I realise it's hard for you to——'

'Oh, please, Daddy!' Tamsyn didn't want to talk about it any more. 'Let it go, for now. How do you like your coffee? Black or white?'

Lance regarded her for a long moment and then he nodded. 'Very well, Tamsyn. We'll leave it. And I like my coffee black, but sweet.'

Over the aromatic beverage they discussed the details of her flight and when the conversation came round to Hywel Benedict again, she asked: 'Does—does Mr. Benedict have a farm or something?'

Lance stared at her in surprise. 'Hywel? Heavens, no!'

Tamsyn tipped her head on one side. 'Then what does he do?'

'Didn't he tell you?'

'No.'

43

Her father shook his head. 'Ah, well, no. I suppose he wouldn't, at that. Hywel's a writer, *cariad*. Quite well known, he is. But you wouldn't know that, living in America.'

'*A writer!*'

Tamsyn was stunned. She remembered with self-loathing the way she had gone on about the cultural advantages of living in the city and of how she had chided him about art and music and books, almost setting herself up as an authority on the subject. How ridiculous she must have sounded to a man who was a writer himself. Her cheeks burned with the memory of it all, but her father seemed not to notice.

'Yes,' he was saying now, 'he's become more reserved since Maureen left.'

Tamsyn's head jerked up. 'Maureen? Who's Maureen?'

'Why, Maureen Benedict, of course, *bach*,' replied her father. 'Hywel's wife!'

CHAPTER THREE

He was married! Hywel Benedict was married. And why should that information mean anything to her? It was stupid—the kind of adolescent reaction he would expect from her. It was only natural that a man of his age and experience should have a wife.

She realised her father was looking at her and made an indifferent gesture. 'Where has his wife gone, then?' she asked, trying to sound casually interested.

Lance Stanford lit a cigarette before replying, inhaling deeply, and smiling rather ruefully. 'Filthy habit, I know,' he said, indicating the cigarette. 'I always recommend my patients to give it up, but I find it relaxes my nerves.' He frowned. 'Now what were you asking? Oh, yes, where has Maureen gone? Well, she's in London, as far as I know. She left Hywel nearly five years ago.'

Tamsyn breathed deeply. 'I see. They're divorced, then?'

'No.' Her father shook his head. 'No, they're not divorced as far as I know. It was a funny business altogether. This chap came along and she went off with him.'

Tamsyn frowned. 'But didn't he stop her?'

'No. To be quite honest, I think their marriage was on the rocks long before this other fellow came along.'

'But surely a divorce would be the most sensible thing!' exclaimed Tamsyn helplessly.

'Maybe. But divorce wouldn't rest lightly on a man of the chapel!'

'A man of the chapel,' echoed Tamsyn. 'What do you mean?'

'Hywel preaches in the chapel on Sundays. He's a layman, of course, but here in the valley we don't have the congregation to attract a full-time preacher.'

Tamsyn bent her head. 'But yesterday was Sunday,' she pointed out.

'I know. But he went to meet you because he knew I didn't want to leave Joanna alone for so long at this time.'

'Oh, yes.' Tamsyn nodded. 'It was good of him.'

'Hywel's like that,' remarked her father, finishing his coffee. 'Now, what are you going to do today? Would you like to come with me on my rounds? Or would you rather go into the village?'

Tamsyn traced the pattern of the wood grain on the table top. 'If Mr. Benedict doesn't live on a farm, where does he live?'

Her father sounded impatient. 'Why the intense interest in Hywel?' he demanded, and she realised, with insight, that he was jealous.

'No reason,' she replied uncomfortably, aware that she had inadvertently aroused her father's annoyance. She was being inordinately curious but she couldn't help it. The man intrigued her without her really understanding why. He wasn't at all like the young men she had had to do with back home, and the older men she had come into contact with had bored her stiff. So why was she allowing her curiosity about this man to cause a rift between herself and her father just at the moment when they were beginning to get to know one another? She couldn't answer her question. She just knew that she wanted to see Hywel Benedict again.

Joanna came into the room before her father could reply. 'There,' she said. 'I'm finished. What are you two doing?'

Lance rose to his feet. 'Just talking, Jo. Come and sit down and I'll get you some coffee.'

'I'll do it.' Tamsyn sprang to her feet and left the table, glad of the diversion. For some reason her father was loath to tell her where Hywel lived and she had no desire to create any further friction between them. What did it matter anyway? She could hardly go and call on the man. Not without an invitation.

Conversation became general after Joanna's entrance. Lance explained a little of the pattern of their lives in the valley, and Joanna suggested that the following afternoon they might all drive over to Llanelfed, her sister's farm, where Tamsyn could be introduced to her step-cousins, Shirley and David.

'David's a little older than you are, Tamsyn,' she said. 'He helps his father on the farm. Shirley's just fourteen, and still at school yet.'

Tamsyn was interested. 'I'd like that,' she said, smiling. 'Are there many young people here? Is there anything for them to do?'

Joanna and Lance exchanged glances. 'Unfortunately not,' remarked Lance, sighing. 'Young people don't want to work on farms these days unless the farm belongs to their father and then they're indirectly working for themselves. But those who leave sometimes come back. Like myself, for example. And Hywel.'

Tamsyn was tempted to bring up the subject of Hywel again, but she squashed the notion. Sooner or later she was bound to see him again in a place of this size.

She accompanied her father on his rounds that morn-

47

ing. It was a glorious summer day, the sun high in the heavens, the scent of clover and new-mown hay mingling with the earthy smell of damp grasses. They drove along the banks of a river, its banks thickly foliaged, hiding a multitude of wild blossoms. Tamsyn rested her arm on her wound-down window and inhaled it all. There was so much beauty, so much colour and excitement, and she thought how delightful it would be to stop the car and plunge into that clear, swift-flowing stream of water.

To reach his patients, her father had to leave the car and cross the fields to isolated farmhouses, and Tamsyn went with him, loving every minute of it. For the moment she had forgotten her home in Boston, Gerry Thorpe, and regretfully, her mother.

Lunch was ready when they got back to the house and Tamsyn tackled the home-made leek pie with relish. Joanna watched her with obvious enjoyment. 'At least you don't have to worry about your figure,' she remarked, smiling.

Tamsyn looked up from her empty plate. 'I expect I should if I stayed for very long. You make delicious pastry, Joanna.'

Joanna sighed. 'Good. I'm glad you like it. How about you, Lance? A second helping?'

Tamsyn's father shook his head, wiping his mouth with his napkin. 'What? With apple crumble to follow!' he exclaimed, and they all laughed. It was a shared sound of pleasure and Tamsyn relaxed completely. It was going to be all right. It *had* to be.

The following morning Tamsyn had her first real look at the village of Trefallath. Joanna had some shopping to do, so Lance drove them into the village on his way out upon his rounds. Joanna explained that they were going to visit Dilys Owen, the schoolmaster's wife, and that she would run them home again.

There was only one store in the village and it sold practically everything that could not be supplied from the farm direct. Tamsyn already knew that her father's milk was brought across from the nearby farm every morning, and Joanna had told her that they got their meat and dairy produce from there, too.

Dilys Owen was a woman of Joanna's age, or perhaps a little older. She welcomed them into her house next to the school. 'Just in time for coffee,' she said, after Joanna had introduced Tamsyn. 'Come along outside into the garden. It's too nice to stay indoors. You won't object to the children playing in the yard, will you? Although they're on holiday now they like using the climbing frame.'

Joanna shook her head and they walked out into the garden at the back of the house. A wicker table and chairs had been placed in the shade of a huge apple tree and Joanna sat down thankfully, glad to rest her legs.

Tamsyn sat down, too, but on the edge of the chair, too interested in everything to relax for long.

Dilys brought out the tray of coffee and placed it on the table, glancing at her young visitor. 'And how are you settling down here, Tamsyn?' she asked, smiling. 'I expect you find everything very different from Boston.'

Tamsyn nodded. 'Very different,' she agreed. 'But I like it.'

Dilys poured the coffee. 'You're still at school, I suppose.'

'I'm at college,' amended Tamsyn, helping herself to sugar at Dilys's instigation. 'My mother——' She hesi-

49

tated, glancing awkwardly at Joanna, but then, seeing no reaction, she went on: 'My mother wants me to go on and graduate with honours and become a lecturer like herself.'

'A lecturer in what, dear?' Dilys was persistent.

'Why, English, I guess. That's my best subject.'

Dilys handed Joanna her coffee and then took a seat herself, offering biscuits. 'And what do you want to do, Tamsyn? Do you think that kind of career will suit you?'

Tamsyn looked rather helplessly at Joanna and her stepmother came to the rescue. 'Tamsyn's got plenty of time to think about that, haven't you, Tamsyn?' Tamsyn nodded gratefully, and Joanna went on: 'Have you finished making that skirt you showed me last time I was here, Dilys?'

Dilys had, perforce, to be diverted, but Tamsyn could tell that she wasn't at all pleased. No doubt everyone in the valley was curious about her, about her background, but Tamsyn didn't particularly want to think about the past while she was here. The house in Vestry Square, Boston, the United States, they all seemed a very long way away. Right now the present held more than enough to satisfy her.

The two women went on to talk about mutual friends while Tamsyn finished her coffee and got up to explore the garden. She was returning to the table beneath the trees when she heard Hywel Benedict's name mentioned.

'It was kind of Hywel to offer,' Joanna was saying, and Dilys Owen was nodding in agreement.

'Yes, but it wouldn't have done, would it? For Lance to be away and his own wife nearing her time. What if you had gone into labour while he wasn't here? What

50

would you have done?' Dilys shook her head solemnly, and Tamsyn felt impatient. Dilys was obviously enjoying making Joanna feel uncomfortable. 'You're not a young woman, to be having her first confinement,' she went on chillingly. 'I remember when I had my William. Only twenty-three, I was, but I shouldn't like to have to go through that again.'

Tamsyn grimaced. 'I should imagine techniques have vastly improved since then,' she remarked dryly, and Dilys flushed with annoyance. Then Tamsyn looked at Joanna, who had flashed her a reproving glance. 'Do you mind if I go and explore the village for a while?'

Joanna hesitated. 'I don't see why not.' Her lips twitched a little as she looked at Dilys. 'You don't mind if I inflict myself upon you for another half hour, do you, Dilys?'

Dilys made an indifferent gesture, still smarting from Tamsyn's remark. 'Not at all,' she said shortly. 'So long as she doesn't get into mischief. You know what children are like these days.'

Tamsyn knew that this was Dilys's way of getting back at her, but she didn't mind. She smiled and said: 'I'll be good. I promise.'

Joanna chuckled then and shook her head. 'Very well, Tamsyn. Off you go.'

Tamsyn smiled at both of them and walked with long graceful strides across the lawn and round the side of the house. The children in the schoolyard were having a great time, dashing about madly. They stared in speculation at Tamsyn, and she grinned at them before emerging on to the village street.

There were few people about, and she was glad. She had no desire to arouse interested speculation everywhere she went. She walked down the street slowly, taking an intense interest in the old cottages that lined it. They didn't have places like this back home, and she could understand American visitors finding the winding streets and shadowy cottages absolutely fascinating. She had met people who had visited the Cotswolds and Stratford-upon-Avon, the mecca for lovers of the English spoken word, but even their descriptions had not prepared her for the real thing.

At the end of the village street stood the grey stone chapel, and she halted, looking up at it. It was a simple, unpicturesque building standing in its surrounding graveyard, some of the tombstones looking older than the chapel itself. There was a house beside it, too, set back from the road, and her heart skipped a beat. If the schoolmaster's house was next to the school, what better place for the preacher's house to be than next to the chapel?

There was no sign of life from either the chapel or the house, and she was about to turn away when something inside her urged her not to do so. She looked at the house again. It was not a particularly large dwelling by any standards and there was a neglected look about it. Was that where he lived? Was it possible? Dared she knock and find out? And if she did, what could she say?

She frowned. She could always thank him for bringing her from London. After all, back home she would have picked up the telephone before now and done just that.

Her feet were moving slowly towards the garden gate. Dare she go and disturb him? He might be working. Writers weren't like ordinary people; they worked at odd times of the day and night.

She opened the gate and swung it wide. It creaked noisily and she looked round, startled, half afraid that she was being observed. But apart from a couple of old men talking together down the street there was no one about.

She walked determinedly up the garden path. She was committed now so she might as well get it over with. She halted at the front door and looked for a bell. There was none, so she knocked.

Absolute silence followed her knocking. She sighed. He obviously wasn't at home. She could leave without anyone being aware of what she had done. Besides, she couldn't be absolutely certain that this was where Hywel Benedict lived. She was only guessing.

But even as she turned away, she heard a sound from inside, and presently the door swung open to reveal a small, dumpy little woman wearing a striped apron and carrying a duster. She looked curiously at Tamsyn and then said: 'Yes?' in rather aggressive tones.

Tamsyn sighed. 'I—I'm sorry, I must have got the wrong house,' she stammered. 'I—I——I was looking for Mr. Benedict.'

'Who is it, Mrs. Williams?'

The low, almost musical voice was unmistakable, and Tamsyn knew that she had not arrived at the wrong door after all. She took a deep breath, and the dumpy little woman half-turned to say: 'There's some young woman to see you, Mr. Benedict.'

Hywel Benedict came down the hall. His thick hair was untidy as though he had been running his hands through it pretty thoroughly, and as it was over-long it brushed the neck of the sweat shirt he was wearing together with close-fitting canvas trousers. The shirt did not look particularly clean and was open halfway down his chest to reveal the growth of dark hair beneath. The strong muscles of his legs strained against the close-fitting pants, and he was every bit as disturbing now as he had been when first she had encountered him at the airport.

When he saw Tamsyn, his eyes narrowed and he said abruptly: 'All right, Mrs. Williams, you can get on. I can attend to this.'

'Yes, sir.' Mrs. Williams cast a speculative look in Tamsyn's direction before going off down the hall, muttering to herself.

Hywel Benedict surveyed Tamsyn appraisingly, making her intensely conscious of her jeans and sleeveless sweater, then he said, rather shortly: 'Why have you come here?'

Tamsyn fiddled with the belt of her jeans. 'I—er—I was exploring the village, and I thought I'd call and thank you for bringing me down from London.'

'You already thanked me,' remarked Hywel dryly. 'How did you know where I lived?'

'I guessed. Joanna's visiting with Mrs. Owen, the schoolmaster's wife, and I thought if the schoolmaster lives next to the school, what better place for the preacher to live than next to the chapel.'

'Who told you I was the preacher?'

'Why, Daddy, of course.' Tamsyn sighed rather resentfully. 'Aren't you going to invite me in?'

'No.' His tone was uncompromising, and Tamsyn stared at him.

'Why?'

'Don't you know?'

'No. How could I?' Tamsyn put her hands on her hips.

'In a village of this size, gossip is the next best thing to—well, to most things. If I invite you in here in less than half an hour the whole valley will be aware of it.'

'So what?' Tamsyn frowned. 'You're not afraid of gossip, are you?'

Hywel heaved a sigh. 'Why did you come here?'

'I told you. To thank you.'

'And now you have, so you can go.'

'No.' Tamsyn was appealing. 'Don't send me away, Hywel. Couldn't we talk for a while?'

He looked down at her for a long moment and then without a word he stepped aside and she walked into the hallway of the house. He closed the door behind her and then walked ahead of her down the thinly carpeted hallway and into a room on the left.

It was a room like no room Tamsyn had ever seen before. There were books and papers everywhere; piled on cupboards and tables, on shelves and ledges, and on the huge desk which dominated everything else. There was a typewriter on the desk, too, and around it evidence of the work he had been doing. There was a square of dull brown carpet on the floor and the walls didn't look as though they'd been papered for years. Tamsyn looked about her in amazement and Hywel gave a derogatory smile.

'Well?' he asked. 'Satisfied?'

'I don't know what you mean.'

'You were curious to know where I worked, weren't you? No doubt your father also told you I wrote. Well, you'll find no exalted aspirations here.'

Tamsyn turned on him. 'I didn't come here to view the author!' she snapped. 'Believe it or not, I just wanted to see you again.'

Hywel reached for his pipe, half buried beneath the papers on his desk. 'Indeed?' His lips twisted. 'I trust the disappointment isn't too great to bear. You should have warned me you were coming and I'd have made an effort to put on a clean shirt.'

'Oh, stop being so—so cynical!' she exclaimed hotly. 'I'm sorry if you find my visit an intrusion. But I wasn't to know that by coming here I'd create an international incident!'

Hywel threw his pipe back on to the table and thrust his hands into his back hip pockets. 'Don't get so heated,' he advised dryly. 'You're here now. The damage, if there is to be any damage, is done.'

Tamsyn pressed her lips together moodily. 'What harm is there in me coming here? It's broad daylight!'

'Scandalous behaviour, like beauty, is in the eye of the beholder,' he remarked.

Tamsyn sighed. 'Well, I don't particularly care what people think!' she exclaimed.

'Don't you?' His eyes narrowed.

'No.' Tamsyn spread her hands helplessly. 'However do you find anything here?'

Hywel glanced round. 'I manage.'

'Do you live alone? Or does that woman—that Mrs. Williams live here?'

'Mrs. Williams?' He raised his eyebrows. 'No, she doesn't live here. She comes in a couple of times a week and cleans the place up, that's all.'

Tamsyn wrinkled her nose. 'Not very thoroughly by the look of things,' she observed almost under her breath, but he heard her.

'I didn't ask for your opinion, Miss Stanford,' he stated coldly.

Tamsyn shrugged her shoulders. 'I know it. But it's

the truth. From the outside this house has a very neglected air.'

'Has it?' He sounded bored. 'But then my surroundings have never meant much to me. It's people who concern my thoughts.'

'Does Mrs. Williams do your washing, too?' Tamsyn coloured under his increasingly intent gaze.

'Is it any concern of yours?' he demanded. 'Now look, you inquisitive little cat, I think you've said quite enough. I don't need your assistance.'

Tamsyn stood her ground, although her legs felt strangely weak. Her fingers itched to tidy the place up, to sort through his papers for him and create order out of chaos. She would have liked to have seen the rest of the house, too. Judging by the untidy state of Mrs. Williams, she somehow did not think she was an ideal housekeeper.

'You might ask me to sit down,' she suggested now. 'That is, if there are chairs under all these books. Whatever do you read?' She picked up the nearest volume and scanned the title page curiously. 'The inevitable rise of socialism!' she read in disgust. 'Do you find time to get through all these? Is this what you write, too? Politics?'

'There are chairs under the books, I read anything when I have the time, and I write novels mostly,' he responded sardonically. 'Anything else?'

Tamsyn felt impatient. 'You're treating me like a child!'

'And aren't you?'

'No. You know I'm not. I'm almost eighteen.'

'A great age. I'm exactly twenty years your senior.'

Tamsyn shrugged. 'That's nothing. Men mature later than women.'

His expression was humorous. 'But you're not yet a woman,' he stated categorically. 'Are you?'

Tamsyn coloured. 'What constitutes a woman?'

He moved irritably. 'Various things that I have no intention of discussing with you,' he retorted. 'Is that all?'

'You want me to go?' she asked, disappointedly.

'I think that would be best, don't you?'

Tamsyn looked dejected. 'When you left the other evening and I asked if I would see you again you said that my father knew where you lived. I thought that meant you wanted to see me again.'

He gave an exasperated exclamation. 'Tamsyn, you ridiculous child, you can't stay here indefinitely. I've tried to explain the situation as best I can. I have no desire to be accused of corrupting an adolescent!'

Tamsyn gasped. 'What do you mean?'

'Well, no one is going to believe that you would want to stay here and talk to me when you might be out with people of your own age, are they? They'll imagine the worst, I've no doubt.'

'But—but you're the preacher!'

'Yes.'

'And my father told me that you were married but that you and your wife are separated.'

'Did he now?' Hywel looked impatient. 'It seems to me your father has been discussing me rather a lot.'

'Only because I asked him to,' put in Tamsyn hastily.

'And you think these things you have said are in my favour? I think not.' He frowned. 'And why would you be interested in me, in any case?'

'I don't know.' Tamsyn bent her head. Then she looked up. 'Can I come and see you again?'

Hywel turned away abruptly. 'Maybe,' he said reluctantly.

Tamsyn sighed. 'Do you come out to the house? To see Joanna and my father?'

'Sometimes. Your father and I have a drink together in the pub most evenings.'

'Oh, I see.' Tamsyn hunched her shoulders, scuffling her feet. 'I'd like to do that.'

'What?' He turned back to her.

'Have a drink in the pub in the evening.' She tilted her head to one side. 'Would you take me?'

'No.'

'Why? It would be perfectly respectable for us to talk in the pub, wouldn't it? I mean, there'd be people watching us all the time, wouldn't there?'

'Exactly.'

'What's wrong now?'

'Tamsyn, I don't know what kind of an attitude you have towards boys of your own age, or even what current attitudes are, but I'm pretty damn sure you're not encouraged to invite yourself out with strange men!'

'You're not a strange man,' she retorted, and then glanced at her watch. 'Oh, gosh, I must go. I told Joanna I'd only be a half hour.' She moved towards the door. 'I'm sorry if I interrupted your work.'

'So am I,' he responded dryly.

They encountered Mrs. Williams in the passage outside and Tamsyn paused to wonder whether she had been listening to their conversation. She seemed rather flustered at their appearance, and Tamsyn looked up at Hywel interrogatively. But he merely shook his head slightly and said: 'This is Tamsyn Stanford, Mrs. Williams. Doctor Stanford's daughter—from America.'

'Yes, I know who she is,' retorted Mrs. Williams, her

arms folded across her heavy breasts.

Hywel looked into Tamsyn's eyes, his own indicating that Mrs. Williams was a fair representation of how news carried in the valley. Tamsyn allowed him to hold her gaze for a moment, and then, as something deepened in his eyes, he looked abruptly away.

'Goodbye,' he said, and she went down the steps reluctantly.

''Bye,' she responded automatically, and heard the door close before she had traversed half the garden path.

CHAPTER FOUR

In the afternoon, Lance drove them over to Llanelfed, and Tamsyn was introduced to Nora Edwards, Joanna's sister. Nora's husband, Malcolm, was out working in the fields when they arrived, but he came in soon after four o'clock for afternoon tea accompanied by David, his son.

Tamsyn was enjoying the outing. It had successfully taken her mind from other things, most particularly Hywel Benedict. When she had returned to Dilys Owen's house that morning to find her stepmother she had not mentioned visiting Hywel's house, and since then she had regretted withholding the information. But somehow, she had been loath to discuss it with Dilys Owen listening avidly to everything that was said, and afterwards the opportunity had not presented itself.

Tamsyn was upstairs with Shirley Edwards, Nora's fourteen-year-old daughter, when the men came home. Nora had suggested that Shirley might take Tamsyn upstairs and they could play some records. Shirley had been only too willing and the two girls had spent the afternoon listening to the kind of pop music that Tamsyn's mother had always abhorred. Shirley had plied her visitor with questions about American groups, but although Tamsyn knew some of their names, she was by no means as knowledgeable on the subject as Shirley.

When Nora called them down for tea, Tamsyn led the way eagerly, and collided with a young man who was standing in the hall taking off his socks. She apologised laughingly, and looked into a rather attractive young face framed by a mass of untidy chestnut brown hair.

'I'm awfully sorry,' she apologised, and then lifted her dark eyebrows. 'You must be David. I'm Tamsyn Stanford.'

David Edwards was looking at her with apparent interest. 'Yes, I'm David,' he answered, before glancing up at his young sister who was hanging over the banisters. 'Are you coming down? I want to go up and change.'

Shirley made a wicked face at him. 'What do you want to change for, David? You don't normally go to all this trouble.'

David looked as though he would have liked to do her some physical injury, and Tamsyn hid her smile. 'Why have you taken off your socks?' she enquired curiously.

David coloured. 'Mam makes us take off our boots in the yard, and as these socks were nearly as muddy as the boots themselves I thought I'd better take them off before going upstairs.'

'Oh, I see,' Tamsyn nodded, and heard Shirley's teasing giggle. 'Come on down, Shirley. Let David go and change.'

Shirley reluctantly complied, avoiding her brother by dodging behind Tamsyn, and the two girls entered the large sitting room together. Malcolm Edwards stood up as they entered and shook hands warmly with Tamsyn. He was a big man, like Hywel Benedict, Tamsyn conceded to herself unhappily, and then firmly dismissed thoughts of him from her mind as Malcolm bade her come and sit with him on the couch and tell him how she was settling down in Trefallath.

Tea was composed of plates of sandwiches of various kinds, buns and cream cakes, and lots of fresh strawberries with whipped cream. Tamsyn was sure she made an absolute pig of herself, but Nora was determined that she should have a taste of everything, and she was licking her fingers appreciatively when David Edwards came back into the room.

He had obviously bathed and changed into cream cotton pants and a blue shirt. His long hair had been smoothed into order and she saw again that she had been right in assuming he was an attractive young man. She judged his age correctly to be somewhere between eighteen and twenty, and because he worked a lot outside he had a healthy tanned complexion.

Malcolm intercepted the look that David bestowed on their young visitor and smiled, and Tamsyn realised that everyone was aware that David's spruce appearance was on her account.

After the meal was over, David suggested that he might show Tamsyn around, and his parents and Tamsyn's father enthusiastically agreed.

'I'll come, too,' said Shirley, getting up, but her mother shook her head.

'You don't want to see the farm,' she exclaimed.

'Yes, I do.' Shirley was aggressive. 'Can't I show Tamsyn my pony, Daddy, please?'

Malcolm gave a resigned sigh. 'I expect so,' he said with a shrug at his wife, and Shirley followed the others out of the room eagerly.

But outside in the stackyard David turned on her angrily. 'Get lost!' he advised her shortly. 'You're not wanted, can't you see?'

Tamsyn made a helpless gesture. 'It's all right,

63

David,' she said. 'I don't mind.'

Shirley made a triumphant face at her brother and then danced ahead of them towards the stables. David looked ruefully at Tamsyn. 'She didn't really want to come. She just did it to annoy me.'

Tamsyn smiled. 'I know.' She tucked her thumbs into the belt of her navy corded pants. 'Oh, doesn't it smell gorgeous!'

'What? Manure?' David looked wry.

'No. Just the smell of hay and the air! It's marvellous! I've never stayed on a farm—in fact I can't remember even visiting a farm before this.'

'Haven't you?' David shook his head. 'No, well, I suppose in your country there aren't such things. They're all ranches, aren't they? Thousands and thousands of acres.'

'No, there are small farmers,' said Tamsyn, frowning. 'But we always lived in the city. I never thought I'd like living in the country.'

'And you would?'

'I don't know. I suppose I'd get used to it.' She shook her head. 'But it's not very likely, is it?'

They had reached the stables, and David went ahead to open the shutters and allow a little light inside. Shirley was waiting for them beside a white mare.

'This is Snowstream,' she explained, as Tamsyn regarded the huge animal rather warily. 'Do you like her?'

Tamsyn didn't really know whether she did or not. Horses had not come into her sphere either, and the way this one was breathing noisily down its nostrils didn't encourage her to find out.

'Is that your pony?' she asked Shirley nervously.

Shirley gave a scornful exclamation. 'Heavens, no!

64

Snowstream's not a pony! She's not even in the same class. She's a farm animal, not a thoroughbred.'

'I'm sorry.' Tamsyn lifted her shoulders apologetically.

'Ignore her,' remarked David contemptuously. 'She's just showing off.' He indicated a stall to one side. 'Come and see the new foal.'

Tamsyn accompanied him rather more enthusiastically. She gasped in delight at the dappled little animal that struggled to its feet at their approach.

'This is Benjamin,' said David with a smile. 'Isn't he beautiful?'

Tamsyn was not nervous of the little foal and stroked its nose gently. 'How old is he?' she asked.

'Only a few weeks,' replied David, straightening. 'Unfortunately its mother didn't survive the birth, so we've been feeding him from a bottle.'

'What a shame!' Tamsyn touched the soft mouth tenderly.

'We've kept Snowstream in here as company for him,' went on David, crossing to pat the white mare's flanks. 'She's not used much now about the farm. Most things are mechanised these days.'

'Come and see Minstrel,' Shirley was insisting. 'Tamsyn! Come on!'

Shirley's pony was a shaggy grey Welsh breed with an adorable expression in his soft brown eyes. Tamsyn could quite understand why Shirley was so proud of it, but she refused her offer to try it out.

'You're frightened!' Shirley exclaimed in amazement as Tamsyn stepped back shaking her head. 'Gosh, there's nothing to be frightened about!'

Tamsyn shrugged. 'I know, I know. And I guess I'll get used to animals in time, but not right this minute.'

She smiled at David. 'Where next?'

Shirley trailed after them around the yard as David showed Tamsyn the other livestock, but remained hanging on the gate when the other two entered the meadow by means of the stile. There were cows in the meadow and Tamsyn eyed them warily, particularly as they had the advantage of being free and unrestrained.

But David merely flung himself down on the lush grass and indicated that she should do likewise, and apprehensively she agreed.

David chewed a blade of grass thoughtfully and then said: 'How long are you staying with your father?'

Tamsyn relaxed back against the turf, staring up into the arc of blue above them. 'Several weeks,' she replied. 'Until my mother gets back home.'

'Your mother's married again, hasn't she?'

'Hmm.' Tamsyn nodded, loving the feel of the warm sun on her face. She rolled on to her stomach and looked down at him. 'Tell me, have you ever left the valley?'

David shook his head. 'I lived in Cardiff for a year while I took a course on farm management, crop rotation, that sort of thing. But I came home every weekend. The city didn't appeal to me. I like it here, strangely enough. Oh, most of my friends have left for the towns, but I don't envy them. I suppose it's all rather quiet for you, hmm?'

Tamsyn shrugged. 'It's quiet, yes. But I like it, too. It's strange—I didn't want to come here, but after only two days I feel as though I've been here ages.'

'The valley's like that,' said David, his eyes straying over her face with obvious enjoyment. 'It's the lack of pace here, the feeling that nothing is worth too much

66

effort, and time doesn't really matter.'

'You're right, of course.' Tamsyn decided David's expression was becoming a little too intent and she rolled on to her back again and sat up, hugging her updrawn knees. She glanced round. Shirley was still leaning on the gate some distance away and Tamsyn smiled at her. 'Your sister is dying to know what we're talking about,' she murmured.

'I know.' David sat up, too, raking a hand through his unruly hair. 'She's a menace!'

Tamsyn looked across the fields to where the purplish shadow of the hills formed the horizon. 'We should be going back. I'm not sure what time we're leaving.'

'I could run you home later on if you like,' David offered, 'I have a motorbike.'

Tamsyn shook her head slowly. 'Not tonight,' she refused gently. 'Maybe some other time.' She got to her feet, brushing down her pants as she did so. 'Want a hand?'

David nodded with a grin, holding out his arm, and she gripped his fingers and pulled him up. For a moment he was close to her as he got his balance, and she could tell that he would have liked to have prolonged the moment. But although in the normal way she would have responded in like manner with the inconsequence of youth, right now she was in no mood for flirtatious behaviour and she moved away, much to David's regret.

They walked back to the farmhouse slowly, talking about things of interest to both of them like swimming and motor-cycle racing, while Shirley ran on ahead, content now that they were returning, too.

In the car going home Lance Stanford made some

playful comment about David's obvious attraction to her, and Tamsyn didn't contradict him. After all, David was an attractive boy, as attractive in his way as Gerry, but all of a sudden Tamsyn wasn't interested in boys. Perhaps she was maturing, she thought anxiously, examining her face in her dressing table mirror when they were back at the house. What other reason could there be for this unexpected aversion to boys of her own age?

It was almost a week before Tamsyn saw Hywel Benedict again. Although she visited the village several times with Joanna or her father she had no opportunity to visit the house beside the chapel, and in any case she doubted whether she would have the temerity to knock at his door again after the way he had reacted the last time.

During that week she became familiarised with life in the valley, and most particularly with her father and Joanna. Her days were never boring. Sometimes she helped Joanna about the house or they occasionally went into the village to visit some friend of her stepmother's; and at other times she went out with her father on his rounds, learning how the isolated farms in the valley depended on his friendly solicitude. Doctor Stanford held no surgery as such, there was no call for it, but the people who needed his services knew they had only to send a message for him to go out and visit them.

When there was nothing else to do she put on a bathing suit and stretched out on the lawn in the garden. The good weather was still holding and she had already acquired an attractive tan. Her skin did not burn as her father's did, and she assumed that this was because her mother's skin was so much darker and therefore less vulnerable.

On Sunday evening it was the accepted thing to attend the chapel, and even Joanna, in her condition, made the effort to go to the service. Tamsyn spent some time in her bedroom trying to decide what would be the most suitable thing to wear, and finally she leant over the banister and shouted down to her stepmother.

Joanna came to the foot of the stairs and smiled rather teasingly. 'Any old dress will do, Tamsyn,' she exclaimed. 'What is it? Are you thinking that there might be some reason to make yourself especially attractive? Some young man with his eye on you, perhaps? I don't think David will be there, *bach*.'

Tamsyn coloured self-consciously. 'It's a long time since I attended church of any kind, that's all,' she answered defensively. 'I suppose I couldn't wear trousers, could I?'

Joanna pressed her lips together. 'I don't think that's a good idea,' she admitted.

'Oh, all right,' Tamsyn sighed, and withdrew herself from the banister, going back into her bedroom reluctantly. All her dresses were trendy and she was sure they would not go down well with the valley folk. She half smiled. What did it matter anyway? She was only passing through. She didn't intend to make her home here, did she?

She chose a dress of Indian cotton with a quilted bodice and a full skirt. The dress was various toning shades of blue, green and purple, and accentuated the curving shape of Tamsyn's slender young body. Her hair, as usual, was loose about her shoulders, but she had brushed it thoroughly before putting on her dress so that it shone like heavy silk.

Lance Stanford drew in his breath as she descended the stairs. He had realised his daughter was quite startlingly attractive, but even he was unprepared for this glowing creature who was bound to raise eyebrows in a place like Trefallath.

Tamsyn was conscious of his appraisal and said, almost defiantly: 'I knew I should have worn trousers!'

'On the contrary,' said Joanna dryly, glancing at her husband. 'You look—very nice.'

It was such an understatement that Lance had to clear his throat before saying: 'That's right. You look wonderful, Tamsyn. But clearly such an exotic bloom was not cultivated here in our common soil.'

There was a wealth of regret in his voice and Tamsyn felt something stir within her. His words reminded her of something Hywel had said about her being a hybrid. She must remember to look that word up, she thought inconsequently. She wasn't at all certain of its meaning.

They drove to the village in Lance's station wagon. Most of the people around the valley seemed to drive Land-Rovers or station wagons. Tamsyn supposed it was because of the precariousness of the roads in winter. She had no doubt that the valley was almost impassable by car in bad weather.

The chapel was quite full when they entered. Most of the farmers from miles around made an effort to attend on Sunday evenings and as Lance knew everyone personally there were plenty of whispered greetings as he and his wife and daughter made their way to their pew.

The service was a simple one, but from the moment

Hywel Benedict appeared, Tamsyn was conscious of nothing else. It was a terrible admission to make, she told herself impatiently, as he made his way up to the pulpit to deliver his sermon, but true, nevertheless.

However, not at any time 'during the sermon, or indeed throughout the service, did Hywel look in her direction, and she wondered whether he was aware of her presence at all. Certainly his sermon was delivered without hesitation as though he was well versed in public speaking, and Tamsyn found herself listening to his musical voice with increasing interest. He was not a boring speaker, and his forthright way of translating the stories of the Bible into everyday situations aroused a feeling of identity in his congregation.

When the service was over and they emerged from the chapel, they found him standing outside talking to a group of people. In a charcoal grey lounge suit and a dark blue shirt he looked rather dark and alien, almost, but Tamsyn couldn't look away from him. When he turned his head and met her gaze she felt ridiculously self-conscious and wondered whether anyone else was aware of her emotional upheaval.

But apparently no one was, and Hywel looked abruptly away as a woman on his left started speaking to him. Lance breathed deeply and then looked down charmingly at his wife.

'Come on, let's go,' he said. 'Hywel's busy. I knew Maurice Preston wanted to speak to him about Ellen's wedding.'

Tamsyn felt a sense of dismay. Were they to leave without even speaking to Hywel? She had been certain Joanna would make a point of talking to her cousin. But what could she do? She could hardly hang back waiting for him to say something to her.

Her father tucked a hand beneath both his wife's and Tamsyn's arm and began to lead them down the path through the gravestones and out on to the dusty road. A cool welcome breeze had sprung up, and Joanna sighed wearily. 'This heat!' she exclaimed. 'You watch! Once I've had this child, the weather will turn cold as winter!'

'Hello there!'

They all turned at the greeting, but Tamsyn knew it was not Hywel long before she encountered Malcolm Edwards' smiling countenance. Nora was with him and she looked with concern at Joanna.

'There's hot, you are, *bach*,' she exclaimed, taking Joanna's other arm. 'You shouldn't have bothered to come.'

'Don't be silly,' retorted Joanna, grimacing. 'I'm perfectly all right. Where's the family?'

'Shirley's at home,' answered Malcolm, chuckling. 'And here comes David now. He couldn't attend the service because he's been in the fields all afternoon and he needed a bath.'

Tamsyn turned at the sound of a motor-bike approaching and presently David Edwards braked to a halt beside them, grinning broadly. 'What timing!' he congratulated himself, studying Tamsyn with unconcealed admiration. 'It's good to see you again. Where are you off to now?'

'We're all going home for a drink,' stated Lance firmly. 'Will you come, Malcolm?'

Malcolm looked at his wife. 'How about it?'

'If you like,' agreed Nora, interrupting a conversation she was having with Joanna.

'Come along, then.' Lance began to walk on, but David caught Tamsyn's arm, restraining her.

'Don't go with them,' he said appealingly. 'Come for a ride on the bike. It's a marvellous evening to be out in the air. We could have a drink later on if you'd like to.'

Tamsyn hesitated. She was torn between the possibility that Hywel might drop in on them later for a drink and the disappointing sensations she would suffer if he did not. In those circumstances she would rather join David for a spin on the motor-cycle.

'I don't know,' she began awkwardly, while her father and the others walked on, and David tightened his hold on her arm.

'Please,' he said. 'I only came to see you.'

Tamsyn looked into his hazel eyes. 'Did you?'

'You know I did,' he muttered self-consciously.

'All right, then. If my father doesn't object.'

David grinned. 'Why should he object?' He started the engine again. 'Get on, and we'll go and catch them up.'

While they were talking to their parents, Tamsyn became aware of Hywel walking down the road towards them. Her heart sank. He *was* coming. And she had agreed to go with David! She felt hopelessly resentful.

'Let's go,' she said abruptly to David, and as their parents had offered no objections David opened the throttle and the motor-bike roared away. Tamsyn didn't look back even though she wanted to. She wouldn't give him that satisfaction . . .

It was quite late when David dropped her at her father's house, but although she had no coat, Tamsyn was not cold. They had ridden halfway round the valley and ended up in another village higher into the hills where they stopped for a stroll. Apart from her sinking depression about Hywel Benedict, she had enjoyed herself, and she thanked David warmly as she climbed off the bike, her legs slightly wobbly as they weren't used to sitting astride.

'When will I see you again?' he asked eagerly, leaning towards her.

Tamsyn took a step back. 'I don't know. When you come over, I suppose.'

'How about you coming over to us? I'll come and get you one evening. We could play some of Shirley's records, and I have some of my own. There's a loft above the stables which we're allowed to use to entertain our friends. I could ask a few others and we could dance. How about it?'

Tamsyn considered. 'It sounds interesting,' she conceded.

'Okay, I'll arrange it. What night would suit you best? Tuesday? Wednesday?'

'Oh, Wednesday, I think,' said Tamsyn quickly. 'I must go in. I don't want Daddy and Joanna to worry.'

'They'll have heard the bike. They won't worry.'

'Nevertheless, I must go in. Be seeing you.'

David watched her go as though he would have liked to have shown her some physical demonstration of the way he felt about her, but Tamsyn was glad he had not. She wasn't interested in that way.

Her father and Joanna showed enthusiasm when she told them about David's proposed party. 'Good idea!' exclaimed Lance. 'Give you something to look forward to. After all, it's been pretty dull for you entertainmentwise since you came.'

'Don't be silly, Daddy,' protested Tamsyn. 'I don't need entertainment.' But she wondered as she said the words whether Hywel Benedict had, by any chance, told her father what she had said on that long journey from the airport. She would have loved to have asked whether Hywel had come in for a drink that evening, but to do so was bound to raise eyebrows, so she said nothing about that at all.

On Tuesday morning Joanna wasn't feeling too well, so Lance suggested she spend the day in bed. 'You sleep this morning,' he said, 'and Tamsyn can go down to the store for you. I'm sure Hywel will bring her home again if I ask him.'

Tamsyn flushed. 'That's not necessary, really, Daddy. I can walk back.'

'Well, if you like,' conceded Lance, frowning. 'Is there much you need, Joanna?'

Joanna shook her head. 'It would be rather nice just to rest for a while,' she admitted. 'But I don't want Tamsyn spending her holiday working for me.'

Tamsyn shook her head reproachfully. 'I've hardly done anything since I arrived. And I don't mind, honestly. Although I've never had to do much in the way of housework back home, I enjoy doing what I can. And it will be quite a challenge having a dinner to prepare.'

'There you are, then,' said Lance, well satisfied, and Tamsyn knew he was glad she had spoken up as she had. Slowly but surely, they were building up a relationship, and familiarity was beginning to weave its own bonds.

In the village, Tamsyn soon collected the few things Joanna wanted from the store and explained obligingly to the gossipy little storekeeper's wife, Mrs. Robinson, that her stepmother was feeling a little under the weather this morning.

'Under the weather is right!' exclaimed Mrs. Robinson, nodding vigorously. 'Hot, it is! Never knew such a dry spell for years. But nice for you, though, it is.'

Tamsyn smiled. 'Yes,' she agreed, aware of a sense of wellbeing that had nothing to do with the fact that when she left the store she intended walking past the house next to the chapel.

Several people spoke to her as she made her way up the village street and she realised Hywel was right when it came to her movements being observed. In the event, she found it impossible to walk past the chapel and turn back again without being speculated upon, so she stopped by the wall and pretended to take an interest in the gravestones.

Presently the door of the house next to the chapel opened and Mrs. Williams appeared. Tamsyn remembered belatedly that it was Tuesday again, one of Mrs. Williams' days for cleaning. When the rotund little woman caught sight of Tamsyn, half concealed behind the wall, she called out sharply: 'Are you waiting for Mr. Benedict?'

Tamsyn went scarlet, sure that half the village had heard that pointed question. 'Er—no—no,' she denied uncomfortably. 'I—I was just reading the tombstones, that's all.'

'Huh!' Mrs. Williams didn't sound at all convinced, but she was obviously leaving, for she was putting on her coat, even though the day was quite hot. She turned and went back into the house again, only to reappear a few moments later with her shopping basket. She came down the steps and as she did so Hywel came to the door to see her off. He saw Tamsyn at once and she wished that the road would simply open up and swallow her into its depths. What must he be thinking? she asked herself in an agony of embarrass-

76

ment. What could he be thinking but that she was deliberately running after him? What other reason could she have for being there at all?

Mrs. Williams came down the path and passed only a few feet from Tamsyn, her eyes eloquent with meaning. Tamsyn moved abruptly, her intention to put as many yards between herself and Hywel Benedict as quickly as she could. But her shopping basket which she had been resting on the churchyard wall tipped in her haste and spilt its contents all over the grassy verge.

'Damn!' she exclaimed in a frustrated voice, bending down to gather her belongings together. Luckily there was nothing breakable and it didn't take many minutes to thrust everything back inside. She was reaching out her hand for the final packet of soap powder when she became conscious of a man's trouser-clad legs only a few inches away from her fingers. Her eyes lifted and travelled up over narrow-fitting denim trousers to a dark blue shirt and above that the strong column of Hywel's throat and jawline. 'Oh—oh, hello!' she swallowed with difficulty and stood up. 'I—er—I'm afraid I was clumsy. Luckily nothing got broken. It's just as well there were no eggs in here, isn't it? I mean, that would have been the last straw, wouldn't it?' She was chattering helplessly, but the look in his eyes was denigrating.

'*Tamsyn!*' The impatient way he spoke her name silenced her. 'Tamsyn, what are you doing here?'

She made a sketchy shrug of her shoulders. 'Like I told Mrs. Williams—I'm reading the inscriptions on these old tombstones.'

'I'm not Mrs. Williams,' retorted Hywel shortly. 'And might I add that Mrs. Williams is not as imperceptive as you seem to think she is!'

'What do you mean?' Tamsyn assumed an innocent air.

'You know perfectly well what I mean,' he snapped, tugging painfully at the hair at the back of his neck. 'Come along inside. We're attracting attention here.'

'And we won't if we go inside?' queried Tamsyn, raising her dark eyebrows.

The look Hywel gave her silenced any further attempt at facetiousness and she obediently preceded him down the path and into the house. While he closed the front door she walked down the passage to the room she had been in on that other occasion.

'Not there,' said Hywel abruptly, passing her and leading the way into a room at the back of the house which had the appearance of a living room. As in the other room there was a large selection of books on shelves that flanked a wide fireplace, empty now but probably very cosy on cold winter evenings; there was a comfortable, if well-worn, three-piece suite in a tapestry design that was rather attractive, and a television set on which were stacked a pile of newspapers and magazines. But for all its reasonably tidy appearance Tamsyn could see streaks of dust on the shelves, and several cobwebs glinted in the sunlight from the window hangings. Obviously she had been right in assuming that Mrs. Williams was no more proficient at looking after a house than she was at attending to her own appearance. But at the moment Mrs. Williams' shortcomings were of secondary importance to Hywel's apparent anger at her appearance.

'Now,' he said, facing her grimly, 'perhaps you'll tell me what you think you're doing!'

CHAPTER FIVE

'Joanna's not very well today.' Tamsyn felt a sense of relief as the involuntary words sprang to her lips. 'I—I thought I ought to call and let you know. In—in case you wanted to go and see her.'

Hywel looked sceptical. 'So why were you hovering near the gravestones?'

Tamsyn coloured. 'Oh, well, I knew Mrs. Williams would be here, and I didn't want to cause any—any unnecessary confusion.'

He regarded her impatiently. 'You don't honestly expect anyone to believe that, do you?' He shook his head. 'If your reasons for coming here were so innocent, why didn't you simply walk up the path and knock at the door?'

Tamsyn squared her shoulders, resentment adding to her failing confidence. 'You're not very polite, are you? I've explained why I didn't do that. What are you implying?'

'I'm not implying anything. The inference is obvious.'

Tamsyn sighed. 'Well, why must I have a reason?' She looked round the room. 'I enjoyed your sermon on Sunday.'

'Did you?' He was disconcertingly abrupt.

'Yes. Is this your living room?'

'You might call it that.'

Tamsyn moved across to the window and looked out on a long garden where there were fruit trees and lawns and even a vegetable garden. 'Do you look after all this yourself?'

'No.'

'Then who does?' Tamsyn turned, her dark eyebrows lifting. 'Not—Mrs. Williams!'

'Her old father, actually,' replied Hywel, his eyes veiled by the long thick black lashes.

'It's rather attractive, isn't it? Why don't you work out there sometimes?'

'Because I have no desire to do so.'

Hywel's responses were becoming briefer. He made no attempt to volunteer any information about himself and Tamsyn felt frustrated.

'Aren't you going to offer me a cup of coffee or something?' she exclaimed. 'As I'm here now, I can't see what harm it would do.'

Hywel studied her expression with disturbing intensity. Then he said bluntly: 'It never occurs to you to imagine that I might not want you here regardless of what my neighbours might think, does it?'

Tamsyn's flushed cheeks drained of all colour. For a long moment she just stared at the ground in front of her, unable to hide the pain in her eyes and determined that he should not see it. Then she crossed the room towards the door, eyes averted, humiliation like a tangible thing inside her. But as she would have passed him, he uttered a muffled oath and put out his hand, his fingers closing firmly about the soft flesh of her upper arm, halting her.

'No,' he said huskily. 'No, don't go. I'm sorry, I shouldn't have said that.'

Tamsyn looked up at him then, her eyes swimming with tears. He was so close she could see every small detail of his face, the deep brown of his eyes which could appear black in some lights, the strong nose, the sensual curve of his mouth, the dark vitality of his hair which darkened his cheekbones. The brown column of his throat rose from the opened neck of his shirt and she could smell the warmth of his body. It was a disturbing moment and an aching longing stirred inside her.

Hywel looked down at his hand gripping her arm and his thumb moved with circulatory probing pressure against her skin. Then he set her free, and thrust his hands deep into his pockets as though afraid of what he might do were he to continue touching her.

Tamsyn quivered, 'Are you angry with me?'

Hywel moved towards the door. 'No,' he said fiercely. Then more quietly: 'No, I'm not angry with you. I'll make some coffee.'

'Let me!' Tamsyn moved after him, following him through the door at the end of the hall which led into the small kitchen. There was a stale smell of food, which wasn't surprising as Mrs. Williams had left no windows open, and Tamsyn wrinkled her nose.

Hywel glanced round. 'Which do you prefer? Percolated—or instant?'

'Instant will do,' replied Tamsyn. 'Just show me where everything is and I'll do it.'

Hywel regarded her tolerantly. 'All right. You'll find everything you need in that wall cupboard there. I'll be in my study.'

Tamsyn nodded, 'Fine.'

But after he had gone Tamsyn looked about her with distaste. The stove was thick with grease and no one had obviously attempted to clean it for months. Her fingers itched to get to work on it, but she dared not attempt it now. Perhaps another day . . .

She opened the wall cupboard. As Hywel had said,

there was everything she needed, but the untidy state of the cupboards appalled her. Mrs. Williams was obviously not doing her job. Everywhere there was evidence of neglect. Surely Hywel could see that for himself. Didn't he care at all?

Before heating the milk for the coffee, Tamsyn scoured the saucepan thoroughly. Around its rim there had been traces of dried food and whoever had washed it up previously had not done so properly. A further search produced a tin of biscuits and a tray, and she carried the coffee through on this.

Hywel was seated at his desk as she entered the room, horn-rimmed spectacles on his nose. But he rose to his feet at her entrance, tugging off the spectacles and dropping them carelessly on to the desk.

Taking the tray from her, he said: 'We'll go into the living room. There's no room in here.'

Tamsyn preceded him obediently and took her coffee and found a seat. Hywel did not sit down. After adding several spoonsful of sugar to his coffee he remained standing, drinking it with obvious enjoyment.

Tamsyn sought about for something to say. Since that moment which she dared not speculate upon when he had stopped her from leaving, she had sensed the tension between them and she wanted to break it, to make everything the same as it had been on that long drive down from London.

Finally she said: 'If I say something, will you promise not to jump down my throat?'

Hywel placed his empty coffee cup on the tray. 'That rather depends on what you are about to say, doesn't it, *bach*?'

The gentler tone of his voice was encouraging, and she went on: 'It's about—Mrs. Williams.'

'Oh, yes?'

'Yes.' She sighed. 'She's not doing her work properly. I don't know what her duties are, I know, but there are so many things she's neglecting——' She broke off unhappily, aware of the hardening of his jawline.

'And why should that matter to you?' he enquired, and there was a trace of his earlier anger in his voice.

Tamsyn bent her head, staring down into her coffee cup as though for inspiration. 'I don't like to see an attractive house being ruined——'

'Oh, come along!' He spoke harshly. 'A bit of dust never hurt anyone.'

'Then you do notice!' she exclaimed, looking up.

'I've told you, my surroundings are not important to me.' He moved impatiently. 'What would you have me do? Dismiss Mrs. Williams, perhaps? Domestic help is not so easy to find even in a place like Trefallath.'

'Then let me do something!' Tamsyn offered eagerly. 'I'd like to help, really——'

'No.' His denial was final, and Tamsyn felt dejected. It was as though he was determined to keep her at arms' length, and this knowledge was like a knife in her stomach.

She moved to where she had left her shopping basket, looking down at its contents without interest. She knew her father would be furious if he ever found out that she had come here twice, uninvited, but that was nothing compared to the realisation that Hywel was not about to welcome her into his home again.

'Did you have a pleasant evening on Sunday?' he asked suddenly, and she looked up, drawing her brows together.

'On Sunday?' she echoed questioningly, and then remembered that she had gone with David, on his

83

motor-bike. 'Oh—oh, yes. It was all right.'

'David's a nice boy,' remarked Hywel, his expression relaxing. 'Like your father, he couldn't leave the valley for long.'

'He's very young,' replied Tamsyn shortly.

'He's older than you are,' Hywel pointed out dryly.

'I don't care. He's still very young.'

'Are you seeing him again?'

Tamsyn pressed her lips together. 'Does it matter?'

'Not particularly. I was making conversation, that's all.' Hywel was depressingly indifferent.

Tamsyn hunched her shoulders, picking up her basket. 'As a matter of fact he's invited me over tomorrow evening. He and Shirley are giving a sort of party.'

'That should be enjoyable for you.' A faint smile touched Hywel's mouth.

Tamsyn felt angry. 'I may not go,' she retorted resentfully.

'Why not? Weren't you telling me on the way down here that you couldn't understand what we could find to do in the valley? Here's an opportunity for you to find out.'

'I said a lot of silly things on the way here,' replied Tamsyn, thrusting back the curtain of her hair as it fell against her cheek. 'I suppose I'd better go.'

Hywel made no demur, and Tamsyn walked reluctantly down the hall to the front door. Hywel went to open it for her, leaning past her to do so, so that for a brief moment his body was against hers. A stab of awareness ran through her and some inner need exhorted her to look at him then, to make him fully aware of her as a living, breathing, female being, with a woman's needs and desires. But in spite of the fact that she had mixed with a lot of boys, or maybe because of it, she had never been promiscuous, and she was too young to trust the strength of her own attraction. She could not have borne the humiliation of him ignoring her, and besides, she didn't altogether understand what it was she wanted of him. She only knew that every time she left him it became a little harder to do so.

Hywel pulled the door open, and a shaft of sunlight banished the intimacy of the moment, but whether he had been aware of it or not she couldn't be certain.

'Goodbye,' she said jerkily, running down the steps.

'Goodbye, Tamsyn,' he replied, and closed the door on her.

The next morning there was a letter from Tamsyn's mother.

Tamsyn had not been able to write to her mother as she had no definite idea of where she might be at any one time, but this letter was addressed from Portland and Tamsyn realised that this was the second stop on their journey.

The letter was full of the enthusiasm everyone was showing for Charles's lectures, and there were little innuendoes about Tamsyn's holiday, making it plain that her mother did not really expect her to enjoy herself. Tamsyn knew that Laura found it difficult to accept that anyone could enjoy the kind of holiday that cut one off from one's work entirely, and in the past Tamsyn had been inclined to agree, enjoying the summer schools her mother had run from time to time, without thought of doing anything independently until Gerry Thorpe had suggested it.

But now, after almost two weeks in the valley, Tamsyn was beginning to see things differently. It was nice not to exercise her brain all the time, to relax completely and put all thoughts of the future out of her mind. And it was nice to associate with people who found satisfaction in their lives and were not constantly striving for greater recognition.

Tamsyn's father showed only cursory interest in the letter, and yet she knew that its arrival had disturbed him. Maybe he was afraid Laura had changed her mind about allowing Tamsyn to stay for two months after all. Maybe he imagined that through a letter Laura could reach her daughter and resurrect the barriers which time and familiarity were gradually breaking down.

But strangely enough, Tamsyn felt no twinge of homesickness. She was happy to know that her mother was happy and enjoying herself, but she had no desire to be with her, or to precipitate the day when she must leave Trefallath and return to Boston. It was rather more complicated when it came to discovering why she should feel this way, and she refused to accept that her reasons for wanting to stay were not primarily concerned with her father and Joanna, in spite of their kindness.

That evening David arrived on his motor-bike to take Tamsyn over to Llanelfed. Tamsyn was ready when he arrived, slim and attractive in close-fitting damson velvet pants and a white lace smock. It was cooler this evening, and she put on a chunky green cardigan to ride on the motor-bike.

David was obviously delighted with her appearance and Lance Stanford looked on rather indulgently as the two young people greeted one another.

'Don't bring her back too late,' he warned David as they all walked outside. 'And don't drive too fast.'

David was reassuring, and Tamsyn felt a warm sense of belonging. It made her realise that no matter how luxurious and comfortable a house might be, warmth was a mental thing, generated by the people in the house and not by their possessions.

The loft above the stables at David's father's farm had been converted into a kind of sitting room. There were chairs and occasional tables for drinks, and the floor had been polished for dancing. Shirley's record player had been installed and when David and Tamsyn arrived there were already several young people gyrating round the floor.

It was a pleasant evening. There were more girls present than boys, however, and as David chose to partner Tamsyn all evening it caused a bit of dissension among Shirley's friends who had previously vied with each other for his attention. David's parents came over halfway through the evening to make sure everything was all right and Nora asked Tamsyn about her sister. As Joanna was much better, Tamsyn was able to reassure her on that score, and Nora went on to suggest that Tamsyn might like to come and stay at the farm for a few days.

'It would give Joanna a break,' she said, making Tamsyn feel rather as though she was imposing on her stepmother. 'And I'm sure both David and Shirley would love it.'

Tamsyn made a deprecatory gesture. 'Oh, I don't know——' she began awkwardly, when David interrupted her.

'Why not?' he demanded. 'After all, your father did say you were here for several weeks. Surely he could spare you for part of that time.'

'It's not just a question of whether her father can

spare her,' retorted Nora sharply. 'Joanna only has a few weeks to go before the baby's due. She should be resting, not putting herself about to entertain a guest.'

'Well, really, I didn't realise I was a nuisance to anyone,' said Tamsyn in embarrassment.

Nora flushed then. 'I didn't say you were.'

Malcolm Edwards looked impatiently at his wife. 'That's exactly what you are saying, *bach*!' he exclaimed. 'What a way to offer someone your hospitality!'

Tamsyn shrugged. 'That's all right, Mr. Edwards. I realise what—what your wife is trying to say.'

'Well, you're welcome here if you want to come,' said Malcolm gruffly. 'But if Lance wants you with him, then you stay.'

Nora sniffed. 'Men!' she said, giving her husband a playful push. 'They're all the same.'

The unpleasant moment was over, but it remained in Tamsyn's mind and troubled her. If her staying at Llanelfed would be easier for Joanna, then she should offer to go. But Llanelfed was so far from Trefallath ...

David drove her home soon after ten. The Edwardses kept earlier nights through the week than they did at weekends because they had to be up so early for milking. But Tamsyn was glad to be going home. After the Edwardses had left, she had managed to continue to enjoy herself, but the remembrance of what Nora Edwards had said was still there.

When David left her at the front door he tried to kiss her, but Tamsyn turned her face away and as she did so she saw a dust-covered station wagon parked before the house. She recognised it at once. It was Hywel's car.

'When will I see you again?' David was asking, and Tamsyn dragged her thoughts back to him with difficulty.

'What? Oh, I don't know.' Tamsyn shook her head. 'Probably at church on Sunday, hmm?'

David looked disappointed. 'What about Saturday evening?' he suggested. 'I finish early on Saturdays. We could ride into Llandrindod Wells, have a meal, and then go to the pictures.'

Tamsyn was impatient to get indoors. 'I don't know, David,' she replied, shaking her head. 'I mean—well, my father might have something planned.'

David pulled a face. 'That's not very likely, is it? Not with Aunt Joanna in her condition. What's wrong? Has what my mother said upset you?'

'No—that is—honestly, David, I can't make arrangements without discussing them with Daddy first.'

David shrugged then and climbed astride the motorbike. 'Okay,' he said, and his voice was noticeably cooler. Tamsyn sighed. She didn't want to offend him.

'Thank you for a lovely evening,' she said, hugging her chunky cardigan closer about her.

David gave her a wry look. 'I don't understand you, Tamsyn,' he said heavily. 'I thought—I thought we liked one another.'

'We do—I do like you, David.'

'Then why are you hesitating about making a date with me? Is there someone else? Someone back home in Boston?'

'Not really, no.' Tamsyn knew that since coming to Wales she had scarcely thought about Gerry Thorpe, even though she had promised to write. But Boston no longer seemed the reality somehow.

'Well, it can't be anyone here, because you don't

89

know anyone else!' stated David emphatically.

Tamsyn was glad of the shadowy darkness to hide her suddenly flushed cheeks. 'I've told you, it's nothing like that,' she denied. 'Look, I must go in. Let's leave it to the weekend and see what happens, shall we?'

David sighed. 'If you like.' He started the heavy machine. 'G'bye, Tamsyn.'

''Bye!'

Tamsyn watched him disappear round a bend in the road and then she turned to go into the house. Contrarily, now that he had gone she wished she had made a definite date with him. After all, there was nothing to be gained from refusing his attentions when by doing so she was merely depriving herself of companionship. It was useless pretending that Hywel Benedict cared one way or the other what she did.

She entered the hall of the house and heard voices coming from the sitting room. But when she entered the room she found that her father was not present. Only Joanna was seated comfortably on the couch with her feet up, while Hywel was standing before the fireplace, a glass of what appeared to be lager in his hand.

Their eyes met for a brief moment as she hesitated in the doorway, and in that instant she was conscious of every detail about him. In a casual navy knitted shirt and cream suede pants he looked big and powerfully masculine, and it was difficult to concentrate on what her stepmother said when she spoke to her.

'Hello, Tamsyn,' Joanna smiled. 'You're back, are you? Did you have a good time?'

Tamsyn took off the chunky cardigan and draped it over the back of a chair, conscious that Hywel was finishing his lager as though he was about to leave. Surely

90

he wouldn't leave the minute she got in. Had he come this evening because he had known that she would be out?

'It was all right,' she responded to Joanna's question now. Then she squared her shoulders. 'Hello, Mr. Benedict.'

Hywel inclined his head in her direction and Joanna said: 'Hywel tells me you called yesterday morning to tell him that I wasn't well.'

Tamsyn managed to remain calm. 'Yes. Yes, I did.'

'That was thoughtful of you,' Joanna went on. 'I'd have been alone this evening if Hywel hadn't come along. Your father had an unexpected confinement over the valley and I don't expect he'll be back for several hours yet.'

'Oh, I see.' Tamsyn stroked her finger down the seam of her trouser leg.

'And I must be going,' said Hywel, placing his empty glass on the mantelpiece. 'Now that Tamsyn's home you no longer need a baby-sitter.'

Joanna laughed. 'How appropriate!' she chuckled.

Tamsyn sought about wildly for something to say to keep him there. 'Won't you stay to supper?' she asked, quickly, glancing towards her stepmother for confirmation.

'Yes, do stay,' seconded Joanna, struggling into a sitting position. 'I should have suggested that myself.'

Hywel shook his head politely. 'I'm sorry, I have some work to do when I get home. I must be going. Give my regards to Lance. I'll no doubt see him later in the week.'

'Yes, of course.' Joanna was about to get to her feet, but Hywel made a quelling motion of his hand.

'Stay where you are. I can see myself out.'

'I'll see you out,' said Tamsyn abruptly.

'Oh, would you, Tamsyn?' Joanna nodded. 'I'll probably see you Sunday, Hywel.'

'Fine.' He nodded kindly and Tamsyn led the way out into the hall.

'Do you have a coat?' she enquired tersely, but he shook his head, regarding her petulant young face rather intently.

'Now what's wrong?' he asked, opening the outer door and indicating that she should precede him.

Tamsyn walked outside and when he joined her she looked at him resentfully. 'You know what's wrong!' she declared. 'You came here this evening purposely because you knew I'd be out!'

'No, I did not. As I recall it, you said you might not go out, after all.'

'But you knew I would,' muttered Tamsyn, tugging moodily at the hem of her smock.

'And you enjoyed yourself.'

'As I told Joanna, it was all right. I'm not particularly enamoured of pop music.'

'Well, it was better than sitting in the house,' remarked Hywel reasonably.

'If I'd known you were coming, I shouldn't have gone,' stated Tamsyn, scuffing the toe of her shoe against a stone.

'Then perhaps it's just as well you didn't know,' said Hywel dryly.

'Why?' Tamsyn swung round on him. 'Why are you like this? Don't you really like me at all? Am I such a nuisance? I seem to be a nuisance to everybody!'

Her eyes were abnormally bright and Hywel's eyes narrowed. 'Why do you say that?' he demanded.

Tamsyn shook her head silently, unable to speak.

'Has somebody said something to you?' Hywel sounded angry. 'Tamsyn, I want to know.'

Tamsyn shrugged unhappily. 'It was nothing,' she denied, the break in her voice contradicting her.

'Tamsyn!' His tone was harsh and commanding.

'Oh, well, it was Mrs. Edwards, if you must know. She—she said that Joanna needed to rest more and that I was creating a lot of unnecessary work for her.'

'Did she indeed?' Hywel sounded impatient.

'You—you won't say anything to her, will you? I mean, I'm sure it wasn't meant unkindly. She's concerned for her sister, that's all. Actually—actually she suggested I might like to go and stay at Llanelfed for a few days.'

'And do you want to go?'

'No. Not particularly.'

'That's just as well. Because I doubt your father would let you go. Besides, from what Joanna's been telling me I gather you've been quite useful around the house.'

Tamsyn felt the ice inside her melt a little. 'Did she say that?'

'Of course.' Hywel studied her uncertain young face with a disturbing intensity. 'And now I must go.'

'Must you?' Tamsyn could not help the appealing note that had entered her voice.

'Yes, I must,' stated Hywel, rather sharply, swinging open the door of the station wagon. 'I shall probably see you in church on Sunday.'

'I shall be in the village on Friday,' said Tamsyn quickly. 'If—if I called, could you lend me one of your books to read——'

'I shall be away on Friday,' replied Hywel, with depressing finality. 'I have promised to attend a conference in Aberystwyth.'

Tamsyn hesitated. Then she said eagerly: 'Take me with you!'

Hywel stared at her. 'I couldn't do that.'

'Why not? I'd like to visit Aberystwyth. I want to see something of the country before—before I have to go back to the States.'

'I'm sorry.' Hywel shook his head.

'Oh, you're all the same!' declared Tamsyn unsteadily, his quiet refusal proving to be the last straw so far as she was concerned. 'None of you like me, or care what happens to me! I'm just a nuisance, an encumbrance, someone who happens to have intruded upon your lives for several weeks, to be tolerated until I step out again!'

'That's not true.' Hywel straightened from his lounging position beside the car. 'You don't know what you're saying.'

'I do, too. Well, you've made your position plain enough. I shan't bother you again. I've had enough of being made to feel like some kind of idiot child who won't do as she's told.'

'Tamsyn, listen to me!' Hywel caught her forearm as she turned to go, securing it in a painful grip. 'You don't understand——'

Tamsyn tried impotently to free herself. 'I understand well enough, *Mr. Benedict*,' she exclaimed fiercely, her hair swinging loosely about her cheeks, brushing his jaw as it did so.

With a muffled exclamation, Hywel pulled her violently towards him, against the hard muscled strength of his body, imprisoning her there, stilling her struggles. Her face was pressed against his chest and his breath was warm upon her neck. Tamsyn felt a surge of exultation course through her veins as the disturbing male nearness of him made her legs feel weak, her flesh melt against him with almost wanton languor. For the moment it was sufficient just to remain there, within the circle of his arms, hearing the heavy beating of his heart, conscious of a sense of belonging.

But her reactions were having a different effect on Hywel. He put his hands on her shoulders to push her roughly away from him, but Tamsyn protested strongly, clinging to him like a child, pressing herself against him.

'Please,' she whispered huskily, 'just let me stay here a little longer. That's all I want.'

Hywel thrust her from him then, his face strained in the pale light cast by the opened door behind them. 'But it's not all I want, you crazy little fool!' he muttered savagely, and without another word he flung himself into the car, slamming the door and driving away without a backward glance.

After he had gone, Tamsyn stood in the pool of light, shivering, hugging her trembling body closely. But she was scarcely aware of the cold. Her flesh cried out for a satisfaction it had not received, and an aching longing in her bones solidified into actual pain. She had never felt like this before; she had not known such depth of feeling, of passion, could exist within her, and she thought with contempt of the way she had ridiculed other girls for confessing to be unable to control their emotions. The memory of the way she had clung to him brought waves of hot colour to her cheeks, and she wondered unhappily what he must have thought of her wanton behaviour. Everything that had gone before was as nothing compared to this, and she dreaded the moment when she must go indoors and confront Joanna.

But in the event, it was Joanna who came to find her, her bulky shadow causing Tamsyn to turn and stare at her rather blankly.

Joanna frowned. 'Tamsyn! What's wrong? What are you doing out here all alone? I heard Hywel's car leave several minutes ago. Are you feeling all right?'

'Oh, yes—yes, of course, I'm fine, Joanna.' Tamsyn pulled herself together with difficulty. 'I—I was just enjoying the perfumes of the flowers, that's all. It's such a—such a beautiful night.'

'Yes, it is, isn't it?' Joanna relaxed, accepting her explanation without question. And why not? Tamsyn asked herself miserably. It would never occur to Joanna to imagine that her stepdaughter's relationship with her cousin was anything more than mildly friendly. Apart from the gap in their ages, Hywel was not the sort of man to encourage an infatuated teenager, and that was what her father and stepmother would think of her emotions if ever she tried to explain them. Besides, Hywel was a married man. She ought to be feeling ashamed, not dissatisfied because he had not demonstrated his undoubted sexual expertise on her, because he had not crushed her beneath the force of his passion and taken possession of her mouth as she had sensed he had wanted to do. Oh, yes, she had not been mistaken about that, but what man would not have responded to so blatant an invitation?

She took a trembling breath and followed Joanna into the house. She hoped she would be able to escape to her room soon. She didn't want to talk, she wanted to think, to feel, to relive again those moments when Hywel had held her closely against him and destroyed once and for all the child she had been.

CHAPTER SIX

THE next morning Tamsyn chose to go out with her father on his rounds so that she could talk to him about Nora's invitation. The subject had to be broached or Nora would think that Tamsyn was withholding it on purpose in case her father agreed. As it was, Lance looked rather irritated, and said:

'Do you want to go? I suppose David and Shirley are more your age group, and I'm sure they'd love to have you. Particularly David.'

Tamsyn sighed. They were driving along by the river and although the sky was slightly overcast with the portent of a break in the weather later, it was very warm. Tamsyn's window was wound down and she had been staring out at the placid scene with an intensity that forcibly banished all thoughts of Hywel from her mind. But now she turned to look at her father.

'Do you want me to go?' she asked simply. 'And don't answer immediately. Give yourself time to think. Do you suppose Joanna would like a break? I have been here two weeks already.'

Lance brought the car to a standstill overlooking a particularly attractive widening of the river that had the appearance of a lake. Reeds grew at the water's edge, and a willow dipped its branches into the current. It was all very beautiful, and very silent, only the sounds of the birds to disturb the stillness.

'Oh, Tamsyn,' he said at last, 'I don't know how to answer you. I only know that having you here, living in my house, is the thing I have wanted most for years! And now you're asking me whether, after only two weeks, I can bear to let you go away again.' He rested his chin on his hands where they lay on the steering wheel. 'I don't ever want you to go away again.' He sighed. 'Oh, I realise that I shall have to. I have no intention of trying to keep you here against your will, or of trying to turn you against your mother. But to ask me whether I want you to go to Nora's in spite of Joanna's condition is something I can't answer. It wouldn't be fair. My answer would be biased. You must decide this for yourself, Tamsyn.'

Tamsyn felt a curious tightening of her throat muscles. It was the first time, she felt, that her father had put into words his own feelings about her, and it was a disturbing experience. This man, this kind and gentle man, loved and wanted her. He was her father; that was beginning to mean something at last. He was no longer a stranger to her; they were not intimates, and yet there was something between them, some point of contact that had to do with flesh and blood and genealogy, that no length of separation could ever erase.

She bent her head. 'I don't want to go,' she said honestly. 'But——'

'No buts!' her father interrupted her swiftly, his face revealing his relief. 'Don't analyse your reasons. Just so long as you're happy here, that's all that matters to me.'

Tamsyn looked at him out of the corners of her eyes. 'You make me feel very selfish,' she admitted, a sense of guilt at her own duplicity gripping her.

'Nonsense!' Lance set the car in motion again. 'Now, we'll say no more about it. I'll have a word with Nora myself when I see her.'

Tamsyn sighed and returned her attention to the

scenery. But she had known all along that Hywel had been right in assuming that Lance would never allow her to go. Only his methods had been different from what she had expected, that was all.

On Sunday evening they all went to chapel, as usual. Tamsyn, who had not seen Hywel since he left her on Wednesday evening, was a mass of nerves, and spent several minutes deciding what she could wear. Finally she chose a dress of cream jersey that moulded her rounded figure but which had to be concealed beneath a cloak of purple wet-cloth because it began to rain as they left the house.

By the time they seated themselves in their pew Tamsyn felt as though everyone must be aware of her tension, but happily no one seemed to notice. And when Hywel appeared and the service began a little of the anxiety dispersed. After all, what did she expect to happen? Probably nothing. She was the one who had precipitated last Wednesday's incident and no doubt he had forgotten about it by now. Unless he remembered it with impatience, of course, like everything else she had done...

When the service was over and they went outside there was no lingering departure to look forward to. The rain dispersed everyone efficiently, and Lance hurried his wife and daughter towards their car, shouting goodbye to their friends as they went. Hywel himself was not around and Tamsyn felt an awful sense of depression descending upon her. She might have stayed at home for all the interest he had taken in her; he had not even looked at her throughout the service.

The following week passed slowly. The cooler weather suited Joanna better, but because of the constant threat of rain Tamsyn was tied to the house and a feeling of frustration at the enforced inactivity began to chafe at her.

One afternoon towards the end of the week, Dilys Owen, the schoolmaster's wife, arrived to have tea with Joanna, and even Tamsyn was glad to see the gossipy little woman. They all sat together in the sitting room and Dilys brought her friend up to date on all the village news.

'Did you know Alice Williams has sprained her ankle?' she asked, and Tamsyn, who had been listening only desultorily, pricked up her ears.

Joanna shook her head. 'No, I didn't know that. Hywel will miss her, then, won't he?'

'I expect he will. Although she only went in a couple of times a week, didn't she?'

'Yes. But she used to take his washing home, too.' Joanna sighed, shifting uncomfortably in her chair. 'If I wasn't in this state I'd go along myself and give him a hand.'

'Now don't you go taking on more work!' exclaimed Dilys impatiently. 'Nora was only saying to me at the Institute meeting yesterday that you should rest more.' Her gaze flickered to Tamsyn. 'Now that Tamsyn's here, surely she can help you.'

Joanna's eyes slipped to her stepdaughter's, and there was an understanding gleam of gentleness in them. 'Tamsyn does help me,' she replied. 'I've not washed a dish or made a bed for over a week.'

Dilys raised her eyebrows delicately. 'Really?' she remarked, and Tamsyn could tell Joanna's defence of her stepdaughter had been unexpected. She wondered what else Nora Edwards had said.

After Dilys had gone, Tamsyn wandered restlessly

about the room, fidgeting with the ornaments on the mantelshelf, picking up a photograph here, a cigarette box there, anything to distract her, and finally Joanna said: 'For goodness' sake, Tamsyn, sit down! You're pacing about like a caged lion. What's the matter with you? You didn't let what Dilys said upset you?'

'No.' Tamsyn halted and turned, resting against the edge of a table, her hands gripping its rim. 'No, Joanna, I was thinking, that's all.'

'What about?'

'About Mrs. Williams, actually. That was who Mrs. Owen was talking about, wasn't it? Hywel's house-keeper.'

'Yes, that's right.' Joanna levered herself into a more relaxed position. 'Why? What were you thinking about her for?'

'Well, what you said, actually. About helping him. I—I've got nothing much to do here during the after-noons. I—I could help out.'

Joanna pulled a face. 'Oh, really, Tamsyn! Can you see your father allowing you to become Hywel's un-paid domestic?'

Tamsyn shrugged. 'He needn't know.'

Joanna's eyes widened. 'Are you suggesting we should deceive your father?'

Tamsyn coloured. Put like that it sounded awful. 'Well,' she began, 'I didn't mean that. But he wouldn't be interested, would he?'

'Wouldn't he?' Joanna shook her head. 'You must be joking!'

'But I'd enjoy it,' exclaimed Tamsyn exasperatedly. 'And I wouldn't be hurting anyone, because Mrs. Williams can't do it anyway.'

'Wait a minute, wait a minute!' Joanna put out a

hand towards her stepdaughter. 'Aren't you forgetting one important point? Hywel would never let you do his housework.'

Tamsyn pressed her lips together mutinously. 'He would if you suggested it.'

'I doubt that very much.' Joanna was sceptical.

'Well, couldn't you ask anyway?'

'I shan't be seeing Hywel, Tamsyn. Besides, Mrs. Williams has only sprained her ankle. She hasn't broken it. She'll be back at work in a few days. A week at the most.'

Tamsyn sighed, staring down moodily at her toes, and Joanna bit her lip thoughtfully.

'Are you so bored, Tamsyn?' she asked gently.

Tamsyn's head jerked up. 'Bored? No—no, that is—oh, Joanna, I just wanted to do something, that's all. You don't think I'm ungrateful, do you?'

'Ungrateful, is it?' Joanna was puzzled. 'For wanting to help Hywel? I don't understand.'

'No, not that. For—for being restless like this. It's just that—well, I can't explain...'

'I know. You've been confined to the house for several days. I just wish your father's work were not so tying and then he could take you out and about, show you something of the country. The coastline is quite beautiful in places.'

Tamsyn smiled. 'Oh, that's all right, Joanna. I don't need that kind of entertainment.'

'Maybe not.' Joanna frowned. 'But then again...' Her voice trailed away and she thought for a few moments. 'Maybe Lance could have a talk with Hywel tonight. He'll probably see him——'

'But I thought you just said that Daddy wouldn't approve!'

'Not about you becoming Hywel's housekeeper,' exclaimed Joanna, chuckling now. 'No, nothing like that. But to ask him whether he couldn't find the time to take you across to Aberystwyth one day, or Cardiff even. And Hereford's not far.'

Tamsyn's lips parted in horror. 'Oh, no, really,' she began, her palms moistening clammily. She could guess what Hywel's reactions to that suggestion would be. And he would be certain to think that she had suggested it all. 'Oh, no, Joanna, I couldn't impose——'

'Nonsense!' Joanna was looking pleased with herself. 'I'm surprised your father hasn't thought of this before. It's the ideal solution and I'm sure Hywel wouldn't mind.'

Tamsyn was aghast. There was nothing she could say, no comment she could make which would convince Joanna that her protests were anything more than perfunctory. But what would Hywel say?

Tamsyn made sure she was in bed before her father arrived home that evening. She could hear the sound of his and Joanna's voices as they talked together and she wondered in an agony of embarrassment whether Lance had seen Hywel. And if so, what had been said?

She could have stayed downstairs to hear for herself, but as she felt sure Hywel would find some excuse to refuse she felt she could not have borne Joanna's indignation, however well meant it might have been.

The next morning Lance introduced the subject at breakfast and Tamsyn steeled herself to remain unmoved whatever he said.

'You know what Joanna suggested yesterday, don't you, Tamsyn?' he asked. 'About Hywel showing you something of the country?'

Tamsyn forced herself to butter a slice of toast without colouring. 'Yes?' There was just the right amount of casual interest in her voice.

'Well, I saw him last night and asked him what he thought.'

'Oh, yes?'

Joanna reached for the coffee pot. 'He's left it up to you,' she remarked, pouring coffee into her cup. 'He said he thought perhaps you would rather have a younger escort. I expect he was thinking of David, although we haven't seen him since you went over there last Wednesday.'

Tamsyn concentrated on the task in hand. He had left it up to her, and what did he expect her to say? What did he *want* her to say? She could guess that easily enough.

'So it's up to you, Tamsyn,' said her father, wiping his mouth on his table napkin. 'What do you think about it? Like Hywel, I should have thought you'd have preferred someone younger. I mean, you hardly know Hywel, do you? And he's hardly a companion for a young girl like yourself.'

'Well, I don't agree,' exclaimed Joanna. 'Tamsyn's not looking for a boy-friend, Lance. She's not wanting to become emotionally involved with anyone. All she needs is a guide really, and Hywel is ideal in those circumstances. Heavens, he knows the history of these marches inside out. He's steeped in ancient folklore. As far as I can see, there's no one more suited to going about with her.'

Lance frowned thoughtfully. 'You may be right,' he conceded slowly.

'I know I am.'

'Well, let's see what Tamsyn herself thinks, shall

we?' Lance looked at his daughter. 'What do you think of the idea?'

Tamsyn hesitated only a moment. 'I—I—I don't mind. If—if Mr. Benedict's willing . . .'

'Oh, call him Hywel,' exclaimed Joanna, reaching for another slice of toast. 'He's not that old!'

Lance rose from the table. 'Well, if that's settled, I'll have a word with him some time and arrange something.'

'We'll see him at chapel on Sunday,' said Joanna comfortably, and Tamsyn's heart sank when she contemplated that it would be another two days before any plans could be discussed.

However, the change in the weather brought another complication. Tamsyn was unable to attend chapel on Sunday because she had a streaming cold. She remained at home, huddled round the fire which Joanna had lit for her benefit, feeling very sorry for herself.

When she heard the car on their return she scarcely looked up, but when her stepmother entered the room she put her book aside and managed a faint smile. Then her smile froze. It was not her father who followed Joanna into the room, but Hywel Benedict.

Tamsyn looked down in dismay at her appearance. Fawn corded slacks, a chunky cream polo-necked sweater of her father's for warmth, her hair in a tangle about her shoulders; what must he think of her? Her nose was sore from frequent use of tissues, and her eyes swam with watery weakness.

'Hello, Tamsyn,' he said gravely. 'I hear you're feeling rather under the weather.'

Tamsyn nodded, smoothing her hair behind her ears. 'It's just a cold,' she replied nasally. Then she looked at Joanna. 'Where's Daddy?'

'He was called away to see the Meredith child. They think it's appendicitis, so Hywel offered to run me home.'

'I see.' Tamsyn linked her fingers round her knees. 'Was—was there a large congregation?' It was difficult to think of things to say with Hywel standing on the hearth before her, big and powerful, and disturbingly familiar.

'Just the usual,' replied Joanna, as Hywel helped her off with her coat. 'I'll go and make a pot of tea.'

'I'll do that.' Tamsyn sprang to her feet, but Joanna made a calming gesture.

'No, you won't,' she said. 'You stay by the fire and talk to Hywel. He wants to have a word with you anyway.'

Tamsyn subsided again and Joanna went out, closing the door behind her. 'Won't you sit down?' she suggested politely, and to her surprise Hywel lowered his bulk on to the couch beside her.

'Thank you. And how are you feeling?'

'I'm all right.' Tamsyn rested her elbows on her knees and rested her chin in her hands, bending her head so that her hair fell about her cheeks in a concealing curtain. 'And before you say anything I should tell you that this idea of you taking me about wasn't mine!'

'Did I say it was?'

'No, but you're about to.'

'No, I'm not.' He sounded impatient. 'How long have you been like this?'

'Since yesterday,' replied Tamsyn, in a muffled voice.

Hywel sighed and leaning towards her he lifted the curtain of hair and secured it behind her ear. His fingers seemed to linger against the skin of her neck and then his hand was withdrawn again, much to Tamsyn's regret. She liked the feel of those hard hands against her. 'That's better,' he remarked dryly. 'Now I can see you.'

'Do you want to?' Tamsyn looked at him then, holding his dark gaze with hers.

Hywel's eyes narrowed. 'Don't be provocative,' he advised chillingly. 'It doesn't suit you.'

'Then what does?' Tamsyn's mouth grew tremulously mutinous.

'Just be yourself,' he replied, unbuttoning the jacket of his dark lounge suit and relaxing back against the soft upholstery of the couch.

Tamsyn turned so that she could see him. She had the strongest desire to touch him, to slide his jacket from his shoulders and wind her arms about his neck; to kiss him, to press against him and let him take possession of her with mindless abandon . . .

As though something of what she was feeling showed in her eyes, Hywel reached out a hand and turned her face away from him with rough insistence. 'Stop it!' he commanded harshly. 'I know you're feeling pretty low, but you've got to stop feeling sorry for yourself.'

'You don't know how I feel,' she retorted bitterly, cupping her chin in her hands again, her shoulders hunched.

'Oh yes, I do, Tamsyn,' he replied grimly. 'I know exactly how you feel!'

Tamsyn looked at him out of the corners of her eyes. 'So what are you going to do about it?'

'Me?' He shook his head. 'Nothing.'

Tamsyn compressed her lips. 'I think I hate you, Hywel Benedict!' she said distinctly.

'Do you?' He raised his dark eyebrows. 'I'm relieved to hear it.'

Tamsyn heaved a sigh and returned her gaze to the leaping flames in the hearth. 'What did you want to speak to me about?' she asked in a small voice.

'I thought we might discuss where you would like to go first,' he remarked.

'Are you sure you want to take me anywhere?' asked Tamsyn moodily.

Hywel uttered an imprecation. 'Stop reducing everything to the personal!' he directed coldly.

'Well, what am I supposed to say?' she asked, glancing at his set features. 'I'm sure it must be annoying for you having to put yourself out for a—a schoolgirl! That is how you regard me, isn't it? An irritating, insensitive schoolgirl!'

Hywel leant forward then, grasping a handful of her hair and forcing her round to face him, making her wince at his brutal disregard for her scalp. 'Stop talking like that!' he demanded fiercely.

'You're hurting me,' she protested.

'Not half as much as I could, believe me!' he muttered. 'What is it with you, Tamsyn? Do you want me to mention what happened between us the other evening, is that what it is? Do you want me to apologise? Or would you rather I repeated the performance?' His lips twisted. 'Tamsyn, you haven't the faintest idea of what you're endeavouring to provoke, but if you want me to treat you like that then you've got to be prepared to take the consequences!'

Tamsyn was trembling violently. 'What consequences?' she whispered, tugging her hair from his grasp with painful insistence.

Hywel looked into her eyes and for a moment she

felt as though she was drowning, her breathing was constricted and an aching weakness invaded her lower limbs. 'The usual ones,' he replied roughly, and then the door opened and Joanna came in carrying the tray of tea.

Hywel sprang up at once and took the tray from her, indicating that she should take his seat upon the couch. But Joanna preferred an upright chair and after placing one for her Hywel took the armchair beside her. He didn't look at Tamsyn again and an awful feeling of despair gripped her. No matter what she said or did he was always capable of cutting her down to size. He had said he knew how she felt. If that were so it should convince her once and for all that she was merely a source of annoyance to him, and anything else was purely wishful thinking on her part.

'Have you discussed where you're going to go?' Joanna was asking now, and Hywel shook his head.

'Not really. Although for my part I would suggest we visited Machynlleth and Montgomery before making for the coast. Do you remember Machynlleth, Joanna? We used to go fishing there when we were children.'

Joanna smiled reminiscently. 'Heavens, yes! The River Dovey. Oh, yes, you must go there, Tamsyn.'

Tamsyn sniffed and blew her nose. 'I don't think it's worth discussing anything definite,' she said. 'Until I know how much longer this cold's going to last.'

'Nonsense,' exclaimed Joanna at once. 'Your cold's much better today than it was yesterday. Some fresh air will do you good.'

Tamsyn coloured hotly. 'Mr. Benedict may not want to risk getting it himself,' she pointed out tightly.

Joanna looked at Hywel, who was drinking his tea.

'I'm sure Hywel's not so concerned about his health, are you, Hywel?'

Hywel rose to his feet. 'Perhaps your visitor would rather not go with me,' he remarked.

'That's not true!' Tamsyn couldn't prevent the outburst. Then: 'I'll go whenever it's convenient.'

Hywel walked towards the door and Joanna stood up. 'So when is convenient, Hywel?'

He hesitated in the doorway, looking at Tamsyn then, although her face was averted. 'How about Tuesday?' he suggested. 'I could pick her up about ten o'clock?'

'That sounds fine, doesn't it, Tamsyn?' Joanna was becoming a little impatient with her stepdaughter's indifference now.

Tamsyn looked up. 'If you like,' she agreed.

Joanna pursed her lips and with a casual gesture Hywel went out into the hall followed by his cousin. Tamsyn heard the engine start up and the car move away, and then Joanna came back into the room looking rather put out.

'You were not very polite, Tamsyn,' she exclaimed sharply. 'After all, Hywel didn't suggest taking you out, he only agreed.'

'I didn't suggest it either!' Tamsyn pointed out abruptly, and then seeing her stepmother's crestfallen face she felt contrite. 'I'm sorry, Joanna. I guess it's this cold. It's making me feel irritable.'

Joanna's face cleared. 'Is that all it is? I shouldn't like you to feel that you have to go out with Hywel just because I arranged it. I know your father wasn't very keen in the first place.'

Tamsyn shook her head. 'Take no notice of me, Joanna. Actually I'm quite—looking forward to it.

To—to seeing something of the country. Is—is it far to Machynlleth?'

'Not really. Just about forty or forty-five miles. That may not seem much to you, used to the roads in the States, but here they're so twisty it can take anything up to two hours.'

'I see.' Tamsyn nodded. 'And what is important about Machynlleth?'

'Oh, don't ask me!' exclaimed Joanna, making deprecatory gestures. 'Hywel will no doubt tell you all about it. I'm no historian, I'm afraid.'

Lance Stanford returned soon afterwards and the conversation moved to more general subjects after he had been advised of Tamsyn's forthcoming outing. Tamsyn was relieved. She didn't want to discuss Hywel Benedict. She didn't even want to think about him.

But of course she did later, when she was tucked up warmly in her bed, her throat burning from the vapour rub Joanna had insisted she rubbed upon it. It was impossible not to recall every detail of their conversation and to speculate upon what it all meant. It seemed obvious that he had only agreed to take her out because Joanna had asked him to and he must be dreading the days ahead continually fencing with a precocious teenager. It was up to her to make things easier by not constantly endeavouring to make him aware of her as anything more than an interested pupil in the hands of her instructor.

CHAPTER SEVEN

THE visit to Machynlleth was accomplished without incident.

Tamsyn's cold was almost entirely better by Tuesday morning and she was ready and waiting when Hywel drove up. She had chosen to wear the green slack suit in soft suede which she had worn to travel in from Boston as it was a cool August day with just a hint of rain still in the air. Hywel, in narrow navy trousers, a beige knitted shirt, and a waist-length navy jerkin, looked dark and disturbing, but Tamsyn determined not to think of him in that way.

On the journey Hywel relieved the tension between them by giving her a detailed account of the life of Owen Glendower, the last Welsh prince, who endeavoured to drive the English from the northern marches. He explained that Owen had set up his parliament at Machynlleth at the beginning of the fifteenth century and that accounted for much of its importance.

Later in the day he showed her the institute which had been named after him, which with its library and museum might once have been Parliament House.

Tamsyn was fascinated. Next to English, history was her most interesting subject, and she absorbed all the information Hywel offered so casually, storing it up for when she returned to the States. It was obvious that he was an expert in these matters and she was tempted to question him about his own educational background. But her earlier determination to remain impersonal stood firm and she kept her curiosity to herself.

Hywel returned her to her father's house soon after five, and with a casual word of farewell drove away. Tamsyn, who had expected him to come in and see Joanna, scarcely had the opportunity to thank him for taking her and for buying her lunch before he was gone, and she stood and watched the station wagon until it disappeared from view. As no mention had been made of a second outing, she was therefore surprised when her father came home the following evening and said that Hywel would take her to Aberystwyth on Thursday.

But again, the trip went off quite successfully. So long as Tamsyn behaved herself and didn't ask too many questions their relationship could proceed along quite regular lines and she found herself getting to know an entirely different side of him.

During the course of their conversations on Welsh history, he revealed that much of his work was concerned in this field, and she discovered that one of his novels was now used as a textbook for certain examinations. She would have liked to have asked him a lot more about his own research, but again she schooled herself to avoid confrontation.

Aberystwyth on that warm August day was thronged with holidaymakers and Tamsyn did not think it had the atmosphere of the past that was present in Machynlleth. But maybe it was because Hywel ran into some friends of his, a middle-aged married couple who he explained later were distant cousins of his wife's, and as they joined them for lunch their discussions were inevitably curtailed. In addition to which during the course of the meal Tamsyn was mostly excluded from their conversation because of the disparity in their ages and of the fact that Hywel's friends clearly regarded her as an adolescent. In consequence, Tamsyn paid no attention to what was being said at all, but withdrew into a world of her own where she could indulge any fantasies she cared to create. She was aware that from time to time Hywel made an effort to include her in some topic they were discussing, but as her response was almost monosyllabic he eventually gave it up.

After lunch, when Hywel's guests had departed, it was time to return to Trefallath, and he apologised in rather stiff tones for curtailing their exploration. Tamsyn made some suitably stiff rejoinder and it was left there. On the journey home he spoke little and Tamsyn wondered uneasily whether some mention had been made of his wife. The thought that Maureen Benedict might be considering returning home caused a stab of pure jealousy to tear into her stomach.

On Friday evening Tamsyn had a visitor.

She was sitting with Joanna watching television while her father wrote up his reports in his study when they heard the sound of a motor-bike. Looking up, Joanna exclaimed: 'Good heavens, it's David! I wonder what he wants.'

Tamsyn got reluctantly to her feet. Even allowing for the fact that she didn't particularly feel like talking to him she could not in all conscience allow Joanna to shift herself from her obviously comfortable position on the couch, and she went to answer the door.

David stood hesitantly on the doorstep, his good-looking face diffident. 'Hello, Tamsyn,' he said jerkily. 'Long time, no see!'

'No.' Tamsyn smiled faintly. 'Won't you come in?'

'Thanks.' David stepped inside and closed the door, and then before Tamsyn could move into the sitting room, he went on: 'Actually, I came to see you, Tamsyn. I—er—I wondered if you'd come to a dance with me tomorrow night.'

It all came out with a rush and Tamsyn halted, looking at him uncertainly. 'I don't know, David——' she was beginning, when Joanna called:

'Come along in, you two! I won't bite you.'

Sighing, Tamsyn preceded David into the sitting room and he nodded warmly to his aunt. 'How are you, Aunt Joanna?' he asked politely.

Joanna wrinkled her nose. 'As well as can be expected, as they say. What are you doing here, David? Or is that a leading question?' She looked teasingly towards Tamsyn.

Tamsyn subsided back into her armchair and David joined his aunt by the couch. 'Actually, I—er—I came to ask Tamsyn to go to a dance with me—tomorrow.'

'A dance?' Joanna raised her eyebrows. 'Where's this?'

'It's in Llandrindod Wells. A young farmers' dance. I thought perhaps Tamsyn might enjoy it.'

Joanna looked speculatively at her stepdaughter and then, getting no response, she went on: 'Isn't it a bit late to be asking Tamsyn?' She frowned. 'Couldn't you have given her more warning than this?'

David moved uncomfortably. 'Yes, well—well, I wasn't sure whether to ask her—whether she'd agree.'

Tamsyn looked up. It was obvious to her at least that David had delayed this long because he was still angry with her for refusing to make a date with him two weeks ago, and he was probably only asking her now because his mother had insisted he did so.

'What David means is he can't find anyone else,' she remarked mockingly.

Joanna clicked her tongue and David flushed hotly. 'That's not true! I've not asked anyone else. I—I wasn't even sure I was going myself.'

'Well, Tamsyn?' Joanna looked at her stepdaughter in some annoyance. 'What do you think?'

Tamsyn shrugged. Her outburst had placed her in an awkward position. To refuse now would scandalise Joanna who thought she had been rude. 'I don't know,' she said. 'I don't go in much for formal affairs. Besides, I've got nothing to wear.'

'Oh, Tamsyn,' exclaimed Joanna reprovingly, 'that's not true. You've got some very pretty Indian dresses. And that's what you need for an affair like this.'

Tamsyn traced the pattern of the chair cover with her finger and looked up broodingly to meet David's slightly embarrassed stare. 'How do we get there?' she asked.

David glanced down at his shoes. 'My father says we can borrow the Land-Rover,' he replied. 'I know it's not very glamorous, but it's better than the bike.'

Joanna struggled to her feet. 'I think I'll just go and see what your father's doing, Tamsyn,' she said, with pointed effect. 'Perhaps he'd like some coffee. Would you like some coffee, David?'

'Fine.' David nodded agreeably and Joanna smiled and left the room.

After she had gone there was an awkward silence for a few moments and then looking up at him Tamsyn said: 'Why don't you sit down? As you're staying.'

David did not comply but wandered restlessly about the room. 'I shouldn't have come,' he muttered with conviction. 'I shouldn't have asked you. I knew you'd refuse.'

Tamsyn rose gracefully to her feet. Even in jeans

116

and a cotton sweater she looked almost elegant, he thought.

'I haven't refused,' she remarked smoothly. 'I just object to being made use of.'

'What do you mean?' He turned to look at her indignantly.

'Just what I say. You didn't really want to ask me to go to this dance. If you had, you'd have done so before this, and you know it. I've no doubt it's your mother who suggested it.'

David flushed scarlet. 'That's not true!' he exclaimed. 'Oh, all right, she suggested I came here tonight. But only because I've been brooding about asking you for days—weeks even.' He bent his head and suddenly she felt immeasurably older than he was.

'I see,' she said, comprehension bringing a faint sense of guilt. 'But why did you hesitate from asking me?'

'Surely it's obvious! You made your position pretty clear the last time I asked you out.'

'What do you mean?'

'I mean those excuses about having to consult *Daddy* first!' he reminded her bitterly.

'They were not excuses!' denied Tamsyn, her eyes sparkling angrily. 'I—well, the whole point of my visit here is to spend some time with him.'

'Oh, yes? What about these day trips you've been taking with Hywel Benedict? Was Daddy along for the ride on those?' demanded David furiously.

Tamsyn was aghast. 'How do you know about them?'

'Be your age, Tamsyn! You can't keep things like that secret in a place like Trefallath.'

Tamsyn sighed. 'I didn't say I wanted to keep it secret, I just think it's a pity if people here have nothing better to do than gossip!'

David shrugged. 'As you're a stranger here, it's only natural that your activities should be speculated upon.'

'And what was the result of your speculations?' Tamsyn asked, her nostrils flaring impatiently.

David sighed. 'Calm down, Tamsyn. No one's accusing you of anything. Heavens, Hywel is old enough to be your father.'

'And that precludes any relationship, of course?' Tamsyn spoke carelessly, uncaring for the moment what she was saying.

David's brows drew together. 'Well? Doesn't it?'

Tamsyn coloured then, bending her head and turning away. 'Oh, yes, yes, of course.' The very last thing she wanted was to arouse his suspicions in that direction. She could just imagine Hywel's reaction to any foolish statements from her. 'All I meant was—well, people shouldn't make judgements like that. And as for the reason I've been going out with Hywel, it's innocent enough. He's been giving me a guided tour of Machynlleth and Aberystwyth, that's all.'

David regarded her moodily. 'I could have done that.'

Tamsyn sighed. 'Hywel knows the history of these places. After all, he writes about it, doesn't he?'

David shrugged. 'Oh, well, if you say so. Personally, I'd have thought you'd find his company pretty heavy going.'

Tamsyn controlled the impulse to contradict that remark and merely smiled. 'What about this dance?' she asked, realising that it was the only way to distract David's attention. 'Do you still want me to go with you?'

David's eyes widened. 'You mean you will?'

118

'If you want me to.'

David moved his head helplessly. 'Don't be silly, of course I want you to.'

'Then that's settled!' Tamsyn smiled. 'Now, come and sit down and talk to me.'

By the time Joanna returned with their coffee David was completely diverted from thoughts of herself and Hywel, and her stepmother regarded them indulgently. She obviously saw their earlier antipathy as the hangover from some disagreement they had had, and was relieved to see that everything appeared to be all right again now.

But Tamsyn cried herself to sleep that night, and it had nothing to do with the fact that she had agreed to go to the young farmers' dance with David.

The following evening was warm and sultry and Tamsyn wore a long Indian cotton dress patterned in shades of flame and orange. David obviously thought she looked wonderful, and even he looked sleeker than usual in a blue suit and white shirt, only his tie striking a discordant note.

There was a licensed bar in the hall where the dance was being held, but David, Tamsyn was relieved to see, drank little, confining himself to lagers. Tamsyn refused anything but lemonade, although she was aware that younger girls than herself were accepting alcohol.

She was introduced to several of David's friends and their girl-friends, and in other circumstances she would probably have found the whole affair most enjoyable. As it was, David seemed dull company after Hywel, and she missed Hywel's experience and confidence.

But David seemed not to notice her sometimes distracted expression, and she put a great deal of effort into appearing relaxed and happy. They drove back to Trefallath in the early hours of Sunday morning and Tamsyn hoped she had successfully crushed any speculation about herself and Hywel after this.

David kissed her before allowing her to get out of the Land-Rover, his lips soft and moist. His hands wre moist, too, as they clung to her bare arms, and she had the strongest desire to wrench herself away. She didn't want his hands to touch her, she didn't want his lips violating hers, but to draw back too abruptly would undo all the effort she had made this evening. So instead she permitted him to kiss her several times before sliding out of the Land-Rover. David got out, too, his face flushed and confident, but she avoided his seeking hands and gained the comparative safety of the porch.

'David, please!' she insisted, her tone lightly reproving. 'I must go in. Thank you for a lovely evening.'

David sighed. 'Thank you for coming. I'll see you later today at chapel, shan't I?'

'Oh! Oh, yes,' Tamsyn nodded. 'I expect so.'

'Goodnight then, Tamsyn.'

'Goodnight.'

David gave her another fleeting kiss and then climbed back into the Land-Rover and swung it about with reckless exhibitionism. Tamsyn waited until he had reached the road and then turned and went into the house.

On Sunday evening however, Tamsyn did not go to chapel. Feeling a mixture of guilt and resentment, she excused herself on the grounds of a headache, and remained at home. She could not have faced another evening with David—not yet, at any rate, but she resented having to miss this opportunity of seeing Hywel. She enjoyed the little service usually and as she had missed it the week previously she felt annoyed. But to go would be to invite David to think that she was eager to see him again, and she was not.

So she stayed in the house, wandering around aimlessly, wondering with a sense of desperation what she would do when the time came for her to return to the States. She had been here four weeks already. The remainder of her holiday would soon be over and then she might never see Hywel again. She could think that she might return the following year, but would her mother ever let her do so? She sighed. She would be eighteen in October, old enough to do as she liked, but what was the point of thinking like that? Hywel wasn't interested in her, and he was married! She was a fool to let herself become involved with him, however one-sided that involvement might be.

However, when her father and Joanna returned home Hywel was with them. Tamsyn was startled and inexpressibly glad that she had chosen to wear her amber-coloured caftan for a change. Its narrow lines accentuated the tall, slender length of her body, and combined with her tan it was very effective.

Lance Stanford followed his visitor into the room, his eyes going straight to his daughter. 'How are you feeling, *cariad*?' he asked concernedly. 'Did those tablets I gave you do any good?'

Tamsyn, conscious of the tablets burning a hole in her suede handbag lying carelessly on the occasional table, coloured. 'I feel much better,' she answered. At least that was true now that Hywel was here.

Hywel himself, after an initial greeting, had gone to

stand before the empty fireplace, and Joanna suggested tea. 'I think something stronger would suit Hywel and myself better,' Lance remarked, glancing at the other man. 'Beer all right, Hywel?'

'Fine,' Hywel nodded, folding his arms across his powerful chest.

After her husband had gone to get the beer, Joanna seated herself and said: 'David was asking me where you were, Tamsyn. He doesn't always attend the service, but he was there this evening, wasn't he, Hywel?'

Hywel nodded. 'No doubt he expected to meet your stepdaughter. What a pity you couldn't make it, Tamsyn.'

Tamsyn only held that faintly cynical gaze for a moment before averting her eyes. 'Perhaps it's as well I didn't,' she remarked. 'I should hate him to get the wrong impression. Or anyone else for that matter.'

Joanna looked at her stepdaughter curiously. 'What do you mean, *bach*? I thought you liked David.' She frowned, and then looked up at Hywel. 'They went to the young farmers' dance in Llandrindod Wells yesterday evening, you know.'

'No, I didn't know.' Hywel sounded disinterested. 'Did you enjoy it?' He was speaking to Tamsyn now and she had perforce to look up.

'Very much,' she replied briefly. 'I'm surprised the grapevine didn't provide you with the information.'

'My particular branch doesn't appear on Sundays,' responded Hywel, with infuriating complacency. 'No doubt I'll hear through the normal channels.'

Tamsyn clenched her fists. 'No doubt,' she said tautly.

Her father returned then with beer for Hywel and himself and iced orange for Tamsyn and Joanna. Conversation became general and Tamsyn, who had been wondering how Hywel was to get back to the village, learnt that he and her father were presently driving over to Penmawr on the other side of the valley to see a collection of old books which were to be put up for auction at Llandrindod Wells, the following week.

'If you hadn't been unwell, I was going to suggest that you might like to come with us, Tamsyn,' observed Hywel, raising his glass to his lips.

Tamsyn took a deep breath. 'My headache's almost gone,' she asserted determinedly.

'Oh, but looking at books wouldn't be a good thing,' exclaimed Joanna, shaking her head. 'Fusty old things! Better not, Tamsyn.'

Tamsyn refrained from protesting further. She had the distinct feeling that it would be to no avail, whatever she said. In fact she was almost convinced that Hywel had just suggested it to exasperate her.

After the men had left Tamsyn felt a real headache beginning to throb in her temples, but she could hardly mention it to Joanna. She merely took the opportunity to extract the tablets her father had given her from her handbag and making some excuse about getting a drink of water she went out into the kitchen. The tablets nearly choked her, her throat was so constricted with an awful sense of frustration, and she stared at her reflection moodily in the mirror that hung above the draining board. This would not do, she told herself angrily. It simply *would not* do!

To her relief David did not appear on Monday evening as she had half expected him to do, and life settled down again. Mrs. Williams had resumed her duties with Hywel, this she learned from her father who had been called in to attend to the woman's ankle earlier on, and on Tuesday and Wednesday Hywel went to Llandrindod Wells for the book auction. Tamsyn noticed with some resentment that he had not suggested she attend the auction with him, which convinced her that his suggestion the other evening had only been made to annoy her.

On Thursday morning therefore she was surprised when halfway through the morning Hywel himself appeared, walking unannounced into the kitchen where Tamsyn was preparing the vegetables for lunch. Joanna was seated at the table, enjoying a cup of coffee, and she raised her eyebrows at his somewhat grim expression.

'Hywel!' she exclaimed. 'This is a surprise. What's happened?'

Hywel glanced at Tamsyn, who had averted her head as soon as she, too, encountered that hostile gaze. 'I'm going to Montgomery this afternoon,' he remarked shortly. 'I have to deliver some books to a dealer friend of mine, and I thought perhaps Tamsyn might like to come along for the ride.'

Tamsyn's lips parted in astonishment. From his attitude the very last thing she would have expected from him was an invitation, and it was with difficulty that she prevented herself from gasping audibly.

'I see,' Joanna was saying now. 'That was thoughtful of you, wasn't it, Tamsyn?'

Tamsyn had, perforce, to look up then. 'Oh—oh, yes,' she responded. 'Th-thank you.'

Hywel turned towards her, his manner aggressive. 'You'd like to come, then?'

'Why, yes.' Tamsyn managed not to appear intimidated. 'What time—will you pick me up?'

Hywel glanced at the broad face of his wrist watch.

'Say about one-thirty,' he answered abruptly. 'Will that suit you?'

Joanna struggled to her feet. 'Of course. You'll have some coffee, Hywel?'

'Thank you, no.' His expression softened somewhat as it rested on the swelling mound of Joanna's figure. 'I've got—some work to do before lunch.' His gaze moved to Tamsyn. 'See you later, then.'

'Yes,' Tamsyn nodded, wiping her wet hands on her apron.

'Don't bother to see me out.' Hywel walked to the door and with a casual nod he was gone.

Joanna subsided back into her chair. 'Brief, but to the point,' she remarked dryly. 'He didn't look in a very good humour, did he? I wonder what Mrs. Williams has done now.'

'What do you mean?' Tamsyn rested her back against the sink.

Joanna smiled. 'Oh, from time to time she upsets some of his papers, or loses some book he's left in a strategic position.' She sighed. 'Have you seen Hywel's study? Oh, no, I suppose you haven't. Well, it's an absolute Aladdin's cave of books. But there's no order or system—just chaos!'

'Yes.' Tamsyn turned back to her task so that Joanna should not see her face. 'I'd better hurry with these. I don't want to have to keep him waiting if he's in a bad humour.'

But she was ready when he arrived, slim and attractive in periwinkle blue cotton pants and a lace blouse. She carried a chunky cardigan with her in case it was cooler when they returned home and waved goodbye to her father who had come to the door to see them off as the station wagon pulled away.

They drove up the valley, past fields of waving corn where the Edwardses had their farm, following the line of the river for a while and then branching off to enter a thickly forested area where the trees shaded the road in places with an eerie arch of greenness.

'I always think of greenness as depicting the primeval beginnings of time,' remarked Tamsyn conversationally, breaking the uneasy silence which had fallen between them since leaving her father's house. 'It can be rather weird, can't it? Especially when there's still water close by.' She shook her head. 'I wonder why.'

Hywel's fingers tightened on the steering wheel for a moment. 'Imagination has a lot to answer for,' he remarked bleakly.

Tamsyn digested this doubtfully, trying to decide whether his comment was solely concerned with what she had just said, or whether perhaps there was some other hidden meaning behind it. Deciding she was being ridiculously sensitive, she nodded and went on: 'I suppose it's all a matter of relationships. It just so happens that green and watery glades send shivers of apprehension down my spine.'

Hywel made no reply to this and Tamsyn sighed, desperately trying to think of something else to say. Then she inwardly chided herself. Here she was endeavouring to coax him into a better frame of mind when in fact after the way he had behaved on Sunday she was the one who should be feeling put out.

She stared unseeingly out of the window. The valley was spread out below them now, shimmering in a haze of heat. Despite what her mother had said she had found the weather remarkably good.

Her attention was captured a few moments later by

a ball of brown ahead of them in the middle of the road. Hywel slowed abruptly checking in his mirror to make sure the road was clear, and then circled the unexpected obstruction. Tamsyn peered down at it curiously as they passed and she saw it was a rolled-up hedgehog.

'Poor thing!' she exclaimed, looking back at it. 'Some car will come along and squash it.' But she saw with some relief that it was already scrambling for the verge.

Hywel made no response and suddenly Tamsyn's temper erupted. 'Whatever is the matter?' she demanded. 'Why did you invite me to come with you if my company is so obviously objectionable?'

Hywel glanced along at her, his eyes hard. 'As a matter of fact I wanted to talk to you,' he replied coldly. 'But I was waiting for a more opportune moment.'

Tamsyn's dark brows drew together. 'Well, why the big mystery? Surely whatever you have to say can't be that important?'

Hywel considered her for a moment and then slowed the car, turning it off the road and on to the grass verge, in the shade of a clump of elms. The slatted rays of the sun flecked the bonnet of the station wagon, while the smell of gorse and mown hay drifted through the opened windows. The silence was almost audible and Tamsyn heaved a sigh. She should have felt relaxed, at one with her surroundings. But she didn't. She felt nervy and tense, and the man at her side was to blame.

'Tell me,' he said harshly, staring straight ahead to where the trees gave way to open countryside, 'why did you make some ridiculous allusion to David Edwards that our association was in any way emotional?'

His words fell into the silence like stones into a pond, the ripples of their passing spreading and multiplying in the still air. Tamsyn was astounded. It was the very last thing she had expected to be accused of.

'I—I didn't,' she denied, protestations springing to her lips indignantly. 'I wouldn't. How—how could you suggest such a thing?'

'I didn't,' he replied chillingly. 'Someone else did.'

Tamsyn swallowed convulsively. 'Well, it wasn't me.'

Hywel turned to her then, his dark features more forbidding than she had ever seen them. 'Then what did you say?' he enquired with icy accusation.

Tamsyn trembled. 'I—I don't know. I can't remember everything I've ever said!' She made a helpless gesture. 'What have you heard?'

Hywel's dark eyes flickered over her with apparent dislike. 'I prefer not to repeat gossip.'

'Just to believe it, is that it?' she asked, gathering a little of her scattered composure. 'You don't question its accuracy!'

'I'm prepared to reserve judgement. When you tell me what you've been saying I shall be in a better position to decide whether or not I have been misled.'

'How magnanimous of you!' Tamsyn was furious. 'Why should I be blamed for someone else's misconceptions?'

'Was that what they were?' He sounded weary, lounging lower in his seat, broodingly examining the signet ring on his finger.

Tamsyn watched him with some distress, her senses stirring in spite of herself. What was there about this man that attracted her so? she asked herself desperately. He wasn't handsome, although she found his strong features far more disturbing, he wasn't rich, at least not in the manner she had been used to, he wasn't even particularly interested in his appearance. And yet just looking at him sitting there, one foot raised to rest on the parcel shelf, the opened neck of his collarless sweat shirt revealing the smooth brown skin of his throat rising from the broad, muscular chest, the muscles of his thighs firm against the taut cream canvas material of his pants, she felt the familiar warm weakness flooding her system, and the desire to arouse some similar response in him became almost irresistible. His tanned forearm was only inches from her hand and an impulse made her touch his skin with her fingers, moving their tips against his hair-roughened flesh.

'Hywel,' she murmured appealingly. 'Please! Don't be like this.'

Hywel looked down at her hand against his arm and then he looked into her eyes. 'Tamsyn, I warn you——' he muttered huskily. 'Don't play games with me!'

'I'm not playing games,' she insisted fiercely. 'Oh, why can't you treat me as an equal? I know you're not completely indifferent to me, I just *know* it!'

Hywel moved then, so swiftly that Tamsyn was shocked into immobility. His fingers curved round the pulsating hollow of her throat, imprisoning her against the back of the seat, a desperate kind of torment in his expression that gave way almost instantly to passionate urgency. His eyes, narrowed and enigmatic behind the long heavy lashes, dropped to her mouth and then to the palpitating rise and fall of her breasts. The lace blouse had opened a little way to reveal her throat and he bent his head and put his lips to the creamy hollow that was just visible. His mouth against her hot skin was cool and yet disturbingly intense, conveying his tortured need of her more powerfully than words could say.

When he raised his head and looked down at her his eyes were frankly sensual. 'Do I frighten you?' he demanded thickly. 'Your heart is fluttering like a terrified pigeon.'

Tamsyn moved her head slowly from side to side as the pressure on her throat eased and became caressingly probing, but Hywel was not convinced. Taking one of her hands, he dragged it hard against his chest saying: 'Feel that—I'm trembling!' His eyes darkened. 'Do you know what that means, you crazy little fool?'

Tamsyn slid her fingers across his chest and deliberately unfastened his shirt so that she could touch his skin, leaning towards him and kissing him compulsively where the bones of his throat hardened the flesh. She had never entered into this kind of intimacy with any male before, but some inner femininity gave her the knowledge she needed. She loved Hywel, she had loved him since she first saw him watching her across the airport lounge, and because of this there was nothing she would deny him.

Hywel's breathing increased in tenor and with a groan he slid his hand into her silky hair, grasping a handful and forcing her head back. Then he lowered his mouth to hers, impelling her back against the seat with an insistence that sent the blood thundering through her ears. But she was young and inexperienced and although she clung to him, her hands gripping the thick hair on the nape of his neck, she sensed he was not getting satisfaction from her trembling lips.

He drew back a couple of inches, smoothing the hair

from her damp forehead, kissing the curve of her eyebrows, the creamy rise of her cheekbones, the hollows beneath her small ears. 'Oh, Tamsyn,' he whispered, desperately, 'you're so young. I shouldn't touch you! Don't make me despise myself any more than I do already.'

Tamsyn's eyes flickered. 'Show me,' she breathed. 'Tell me what you want me to do.'

Hywel studied her for a long disturbing moment and then his expression became bitter. 'No,' he muttered grimly. 'Don't ask me.'

Tamsyn's eyes widened. 'Hywel,' she pleaded, framing his face between her two hands, 'don't stop now.'

Hywel's hands slid down her back to her waist and as though that arching warmth of her body was some kind of ignition to his senses she felt his whole body shudder. 'Dear God, Tamsyn,' he said against her nape, 'I want you!' His thumbs tipped her chin back. 'Open your mouth,' he told her urgently, and as her lips parted his mouth covered hers.

And now she knew why those earlier caresses had been so unfulfilling. The hungry demand of Hywel's mouth was an aching vortex into which she wanted to submerge herself, the compelling pressure of his warm body translated itself into actual longing inside her that she had not been aware existed. There was a mindless lethargy in her bones that only complete surrender would assuage, and when decency compelled him to draw back she wound her arms more closely round his neck, her lips clinging to his.

But Hywel knew so much better than she what this kind of lovemaking was leading to. He had aroused her now and it was she who was no longer in control of her emotions. He wanted her so much it was agony, but a stab of remorse tore through him and wrenching her arms from his neck he propelled her roughly away from him. Then he thrust open his door and climbed out, away from the destructive intimacy that urged him to take what she so innocently offered.

He took long deep breaths of air while Tamsyn turned her hot face into the cool leather of her seat, feeling her drugged senses slowly beginning to reassert themselves. A terrible awareness of the seriousness of what had happened assailed her. What had she been thinking of? How could she have thrown herself at him so blatantly, showing complete and utter disregard for the fact that he was married? Her breath came in little gulps; if Hywel had not chosen to extricate himself at that moment, her recklessness would have driven him beyond the edge of reason...

With trembling fingers she fastened her blouse, and smoothed the glorious tangle of her hair. She wished she smoked. A cigarette would have been very welcome just then. It would have given her something to do.

As it was she could only look at Hywel's broad back, at the rough vitality of the hair that grew low on his neck, at the masculine strength of him which she had perhaps denied herself for ever.

Knowing she could not sit there indefinitely waiting for him to say something, she climbed out of the vehicle and approached him. Spreading out her hands in front of her, she said:

'I'm sorry, I'm sorry. I—I don't know what came over me. I'm sorry, Hywel.'

He turned to her then, his face controlled, his expression remote. 'Don't apologise,' he replied harshly. 'It's I who should be apologising to you.'

Tamsyn's eyes widened, her mouth soft and sensitive, even now showing by its tender vulnerability that only recently it had been passionately possessed. 'Why should you apologise to me?' she asked innocently. 'I was to blame. I—I—made—you——'

'You *made me* do nothing!' Hywel contradicted her fiercely. 'Dear God, Tamsyn, surely you've realised I love you! I've loved you since that day you stood in the airport lounge and asked so nervously to see my credentials!'

Tamsyn glowed. There was no other word to describe the light that seemed to envelop her. 'Oh, Hywel!' she breathed huskily. 'Then——'

'Wait!' As she would have moved closer to him he took a step backward. 'Don't say anything more, Tamsyn!' he muttered abruptly. 'Having told you that, having excused myself on those grounds, what I have to say now becomes easier.' He tried to ignore the troubled doubt that was replacing the gleam of light in her eyes and pressed on: 'No matter what my feelings are for you, this association—our relationship—can never go any further!'

Tamsyn stared at him. 'Because—because of your wife?' she asked, dully.

Hywel tugged at the hair at the back of his neck. 'No, not just because of that. Tamsyn, even if I were free, I would never ask you to marry me, do you understand?'

CHAPTER EIGHT

TAMSYN swallowed with obvious difficulty. 'But—but why?' she stammered. 'You—you just said——'

'That I love you? I do.'

'And I love you, so——'

'You *think* you do,' Hywel amended heavily.

'I don't think. I *know*!' Tamsyn's cry was agonised.

Hywel heaved a sigh. 'Tamsyn, stop it! You're not old enough to know a thing like that. Good lord, I've no doubt that before you came to Wales there was some young man back in Boston who meant just as much to you then as you think I do now!'

'No. That's not true!'

'You're telling me you didn't have any boy-friends?' Hywel was sceptical.

Tamsyn coloured. 'No, I'm not saying that. I—naturally I had boy-friends.'

'There you are, then.'

'But they were not like this,' she cried fiercely. 'They were youths——'

'Suitable escorts for a girl of your age, *bach*!' remarked Hywel dryly.

'No. No, they were not!' Tamsyn sought about for some way to make him believe her. 'Until I came here, I didn't care a great deal for anyone. They were friends! My mother didn't encourage anything else.'

'And rightly so.'

'Hywel, I've never felt this way about anyone before! No one has ever—kissed me—like that——'

Hywel's lips twisted. 'Oh, I believe you,' he returned

savagely, a feeling of self-loathing making him want to lash out at her for being the cause of that feeling. 'However, much as I hate to disillusion you, I have kissed a woman like that before, and with just as much enjoyment!'

Tamsyn gasped. 'How—how can you say you love me and then say a thing like that to me?' She felt the burning heat of tears behind her eyes. 'Why are you being like this? Why are you trying to hurt me—to make me hate you?'

Hywel caught her by the shoulders then, shaking her a little. 'For God's sake, Tamsyn, it's because I love you that I'm telling you!' he snarled. 'How do you think—*Mummy*—would react to a man of her own age marrying her daughter?'

'You—you're not as old as Mummy.'

'Pretty damn near!' he retorted harshly. 'Oh, Tamsyn, don't make it any more difficult than it already is!' He thrust her abruptly away from him. 'And as you pointed out, there is still my wife.'

Tamsyn was pale. 'You—you could get a divorce,' she ventured.

'To marry you? I think not. I somehow don't think your father would appreciate me as a son-in-law.'

'Daddy likes you, you know he does.'

'As a friend, yes. As his daughter's husband, no.'

'Hywel, please——' Tamsyn was appealing.

But Hywel had had enough. Without another word he turned and walked back to the station wagon. Climbing inside, he commanded her to get in, too. 'I still have these books to deliver to the dealer in Montgomery,' he said, and Tamsyn was forced to comply, an aching head adding to her mental miseries.

Montgomery, she found, was a far cry from her ideas

of what a county town might be. Small, and not easily accessible, it nestled at the foot of the mountains, a charming little place with architecture of several periods mingling in comfortable confusion. Tamsyn would have liked the opportunity to explore its narrow streets, but Hywel was in no mood to linger. He left her in the car while he entered the bookshop owned by his colleague, and when he emerged some fifteen minutes later, he got back into the car and drove immediately out of town again.

They had not spoken since entering the vehicle, and Tamsyn's feelings were taut and raw. She couldn't believe Hywel could be so blind as to imagine her feelings for him were likely to change. She had never been a girl to give her love carelessly, even her own father had not aroused affection in her until recently, and her mother had never encouraged that kind of relationship. Laura was a cold woman in many ways, and Tamsyn felt sure all these things contributed to the break-up of her parents' marriage. And until recently, she had thought herself like her mother in this respect. Only now was she suffering the consequences of this disillusionment.

It was late afternoon when they came down the valley again and approached her father's house. Tamsyn knew Joanna would be surprised to see them back so soon. She would naturally expect Hywel to give Tamsyn a guided tour of Montgomery before returning home in the evening.

Hywel stopped at the gate as usual for Tamsyn to get out, but something made her say: 'Won't you come in for a drink?' in a rather subdued voice.

Hywel looked as though he was about to refuse and then he capitulated. 'All right,' he agreed expressionlessly, and a surge of hope washed over her.

She got out carefully, collecting her chunky cardigan which had not been worn from the back seat, and then preceded him up the path to the house. She glanced round once at him, encountering his brooding gaze, and a thrill of excitement sped along her veins. He loved her. Whatever else happened, she must remember that.

The porch door was not open as it usually was at this hour of the day, but Tamsyn saw nothing strange about this. Maybe Joanna was having a bath and didn't want any callers. But the door gave to the turning of the handle and they entered the hall.

Tamsyn frowned. The house was unusually quiet. 'Joanna!' she called. 'Joanna, we're back!'

No sound but the echo of her own voice came back to her and she turned anxiously to Hywel. 'You—you don't think anything's wrong, do you?' she breathed.

Hywel hesitated a moment and then went past Tamsyn to open the door of the living room. It was empty, and with determined thoroughness he opened the doors of all the rooms on the ground floor, with the same result. Tamsyn watched him, a hand pressed to her mouth, and with a shrug he went to the stairs and mounted them two at a time, calling Joanna's name.

Tamsyn stood nervously in the hall. What could have happened? Was something wrong? On rather unsteady legs she entered the living room to await Hywel's return, but as she approached the empty fireplace she saw a note propped beside the clock which Hywel had not noticed earlier.

She read it swiftly and then ran to the door. 'Hywel!' she called. 'Hywel, it's all right. I've found a note from Daddy.'

Hywel came down the stairs slowly. 'What does it say?'

'It says that Joanna's started the baby and he's taken her to the hospital in Penmawron.'

Hywel frowned. 'I understood Joanna was to have the baby at home.'

Tamsyn stared at him. 'Oh—oh, yes! I—I didn't think. Do you—do you think she's going to be all right? Do you think there are complications?' Her eyes were anxious.

Hywel sighed, glancing round. 'Now don't go getting the wrong idea. There might be some perfectly simple explanation why your father should have considered it necessary to take her to hospital.' He frowned. 'Would you like me to run you into Penmawron?'

Tamsyn made a helpless gesture. 'Would you?'

'Of course.' Hywel was polite.

Tamsyn hesitated. 'It's late. Perhaps we should telephone first.'

'If you like.' He was indifferent.

Hywel went into the living room while Tamsyn rang the hospital. She was lucky enough to be able to speak to her father and he sounded reassuring, if a little weary.

'Yes,' he said, rather tiredly, 'everything is going well now. The baby should be born within the next hour.'

'Oh, that's marvellous!' Tamsyn guessed how relieved he must be. 'But I thought Joanna was to have the baby at home.'

'She was.' Her father sighed heavily. 'Fortunately I was there this afternoon when—certain complications necessitated her removal to hospital.'

Tamsyn wondered what these complications might

be, but refrained from questioning him right now. 'Well, I'm glad everything seems to be okay now,' she said.

'Oh, yes. As I say, everything's fine.' Her father sounded confident. 'But, Tamsyn, I'm glad you've rung, because I wanted to speak to you.'

'Do you want me to come over?'

'Er—no. Not right now.' He hesitated. 'I'll ring you as soon as I have definite news.'

'All right.'

'But—well, is Hywel still with you?'

'Yes.'

'Then could I have a word with him?'

'Of course.' Tamsyn bit her lip. 'Just a moment. I'll get him.' She put down the phone and went to the living room door. 'Hywel, Daddy wants to speak to you.'

Hywel turned from his contemplation of the garden through the window. 'Very well.'

He passed her and she entered the room, waiting impatiently to find out why her father wanted to speak to Hywel. She half expected her father to call her back to the phone, but he didn't. Hywel rang off before coming back to her.

'Well?' she said. 'What did Daddy want?'

Hywel regarded her tolerantly. 'How do you know it wasn't private?'

Tamsyn sighed. 'Well, was it?'

'Actually, no.' Hywel thrust his hands deep into his hip pockets. 'He just wanted me to agree to run you up to Nora's for the night.'

Tamsyn gasped. 'Joanna's sister's?'

'That's right.'

'But why should I want to go up there?'

'Because your father won't be home until morning and you can't stay here alone.'

'Why can't I? I'm not a child!'

'Lance knew you'd say this. That's why he wanted me to tell you, so that there'd be no argument.'

'Well, there will be an argument!' stated Tamsyn heatedly. 'I have no intention of leaving here to go up to the Edwards's farm. I'm perfectly capable of looking after myself.'

'Nevertheless, you are going.'

'Are you going to make me?' Tamsyn regarded him mockingly. 'How? By brute force? You'll have to, you know.'

Hywel's expression became impatient. 'Tamsyn, listen to me! Joanna haemorrhaged this afternoon. That was why your father had to rush her into hospital like that!' Ignoring Tamsyn's pale cheeks, he went on ruthlessly: 'Don't you think after all he's been through, he deserves a bit of consideration?'

Tamsyn hesitated. 'I don't see why my staying here or not should concern him unduly. So far as he's concerned, you've discharged your duty. He'll be none the wiser whatever I decide to do.'

Hywel breathed deeply. 'Tamsyn, I'm asking you. Please!'

'No!' Tamsyn turned away. The very last thing she wanted was to be thrust into close proximity with David after this afternoon's events.

Hywel looked as though he would have liked to have picked her up and carried her out to the station wagon, but she knew he would not do that. He could not be sure how she would react at the other end of their journey.

'Very well,' he said, through clenched teeth. 'And

how do you suppose your father will feel if he rings the Edwardses to tell you that Joanna has had the baby? And you're not there!'

Tamsyn's brows drew together. 'Well, he said she'd have it soon now. He's sure to ring here if I'm not at Nora's and I shall simply explain that I haven't left yet. That will be the truth in any case.'

Hywel looked at her for a long moment, bringing the warm colour to her cheeks, and then abruptly he turned away. 'Have it your own way!' he snapped grimly, and turning on his heel he walked out of the house.

Tamsyn heard his station wagon drive away with some misgivings. Not that she regretted refusing going to the Edwards's, but it had been such a strange afternoon and she felt entirely disorientated. She wished she had been able to suggest that he stay and share a meal with her, but she knew if she had done so he would have refused in the present circumstances.

So instead she went into the kitchen and put on the kettle and made herself a pot of tea, having only a sandwich in lieu of a meal. She wasn't particularly hungry, but the hollow feeling inside her was making her feel sick and the sandwich served its purpose.

Afterwards, she wandered restlessly round the house, wishing her father would hurry up and phone. If he waited too late it would become obvious to him that she had no intention of leaving for the Edwards's.

The sultry afternoon had given way to a cloudy evening and from the blue-blackness of the clouds that were rolling in from the hills Tamsyn guessed they were going to have some rain. As though to prove her supposition, a low rumble of thunder echoed round the valley and a few drops of rain splattered the windows.

She glanced at her watch. It was after seven. When was her father going to phone?

The sudden shrill pealing of the telephone bell startled her and she rushed out into the hall eagerly. Her father at the other end seemed less concerned with her whereabouts than with conveying the news that Joanna had had a son. Tamsyn was delighted for him, astonished at the almost stammering excitement her father displayed. The child had been born about half an hour ago, he said, and both it and Joanna were doing well.

'I'm so glad,' said Tamsyn again, feeling an unexpected prick of tears at her father's obvious pride.

Eventually Lance calmed down a little, sufficiently so to question why she had not been at the Edwards's when he rang there first.

'I—er—I thought I'd have a meal first,' she temporised carefully. 'Don't worry, Daddy. Everything's under control here.'

'Good, good!' Lance was still too exhilarated to make any protestations at her alteration of his plans, and she felt satisfied when he rang off that the last person he would worry about was her.

Even so, when the call was over and the remainder of the evening and the night stretched ahead of her to oblivion, Tamsyn felt the first twinges of uncertainty. Maybe if the weather had remained calm and unruffled she would have felt less edgy, but the storm was threatening in earnest now and for all it was not yet eight o'clock, it was dark enough to require lights.

Sighing, she drew the curtains. If there was to be lightning she didn't want to see it. She wasn't unnecessarily scared of storms, but similarly she did not revel in them.

Taking a book from the shelf, she seated herself on the couch and endeavoured to apply herself to the story. But too many things had happened for her to relax completely, and although the book was interesting she could not lose herself in it.

The storm broke violently, the sound of the thunder echoing and re-echoing round the hills, the rain lashing against the panes with concerted violence. At nine o'clock Tamsyn went round the house checking that all the doors were locked and that the windows were firmly closed against the wet. The lightning which had not been visible behind the curtains in the living room illuminated the hall and staircase and she was glad to regain the comparative security of her chair. She had not attempted to use the television, afraid of causing a power blackout, and by ten o'clock she decided to go to bed. Once she was asleep, the morning would soon come round, and with it, daylight.

She was climbing into bed when she heard the sound outside. At first she thought she was mistaken, that she had imagined the crunching of gravel under a heavy footstep, but a repetition of the noise convinced her that someone was out there.

Immediately, her heart palpitated wildly, and a terrified feeling of being cut off from human contact overwhelmed her. She had definitely not heard a car, so whoever was out there had come on foot. A tramp perhaps, she thought uneasily, looking for shelter from the storm.

Turning out her bedroom light so that whoever it was would not see her silhouette when she opened her bedroom door, she crept silently down the stairs to the hall. The telephone stood there and she regarded it doubtfully. Should she ring Hywel and tell him that she thought there was an intruder outside, or would he merely ridicule her anxiety? Who else could she ring?

An ominous silence had descended upon the house broken only by the sound of the rain which seemed to be slowing gradually. She breathed deeply. Perhaps she had been mistaken after all. Perhaps it had been a cat or some other wild creature venturing close to the house, driven by the wildness of the weather. She sighed. She was a fool, standing here, imagining the worst.

A sudden crash of thunder almost overhead made her jump and as it was followed almost immediately by a vivid flash of lightning and another heavy rumble the hall and the area immediately outside the front door were illuminated for a shocked moment. And in that moment, through the frosted glass of the hall windows, Tamsyn distinguished the unmistakable outline of a man.

Her heart pounded so loudly she felt certain it was audible. With trembling fingers she reached for the phone, lifting the receiver and putting it to her ear. But it was dead! Absolutely and utterly dead! She rattled it frantically, but to no avail; for one reason or another the telephone was no longer working.

And then, as she shrank back against the stairs, there was a heavy hammering on the front door.

For a few moments Tamsyn remained motionless, too terrified to make an effort to escape upstairs and lock herself into her room, even supposing she had had a key. She blamed herself bitterly for not taking Hywel's advice and going up to the Edwards's, but how was she to know that tonight of all nights they'd have a prowler?

The hammering came again and with it Hywel's voice shouting impatiently: 'Tamsyn! Open up! I know you're not asleep! I saw your light as I came up the drive. Come on! I'm getting soaked to the skin out here!'

Tamsyn went weak at the knees. *It was Hywel!* He had come back!

She stumbled to the door and wrenched back the bolt she had secured earlier, and as she did so a feeling of anger welled up inside her, replacing her relief. How dared he come here at this time of night just to frighten her like this?

She turned the key reluctantly now, but before she could stop him Hywel took hold of the handle and thrust open the door, entering quickly and slamming it behind him. He unfastened the thigh-length overcoat he was wearing and shook the drops of water from his thick hair. Then after one look at her tremulously indignant face, belied by the paleness of her cheeks and the anxious brilliance of her eyes, he uttered a muffled oath and pulled her into his arms, hugging her close against his warm body.

Tamsyn wanted to resist, but his nearness, the clean male smell of him, was too much for her, and she wrapped her arms round his waist, pressing herself against him.

Desire stirred unwillingly inside him, and with determination he put her away from him again, summoning his anger. 'I told you you shouldn't have stayed here alone. Go and get dressed and I'll take you up to Nora's.'

Tamsyn stared at him, swaying a little. 'I have no intention of going up to Nora's,' she stated unsteadily.

'Just—just because you come creeping up here, terrifying the life out of me, doesn't mean that I have to do as you say!'

Hywel's expression hardened. 'I did not come *creeping* up here!' he denied coldly.

'But you didn't come in the car, did you?' Tamsyn was angry too, now.

'No. I walked,' he agreed bleakly.

'Why? Why walk in the pouring rain unless you wanted to frighten me?'

Hywel raked a hand through his wet hair. 'Because, you ridiculous child, I wanted to protect your reputation!'

'*My reputation!*' Tamsyn was sceptical. 'I don't understand.'

Hywel made an impatient gesture. 'If anyone was to see my car parked outside here at this time of night with your father and Joanna away there would be plenty to talk about, wouldn't there?'

Tamsyn hesitated. 'I didn't ask you to come,' she said at last with some resentment. 'Why did you?'

'Have you tried to use the telephone?'

'Y—yes. Just now, actually. When—when I thought you were a prowler.'

'And?'

'It's dead.'

'Precisely. The wires are down over the valley. The storm, of course, is responsible.'

'I see.' Tamsyn moved her head up and down slowly. 'And you thought that—that——'

'That you might try to use the phone and be frightened when you got no reply,' finished Hywel grimly. 'Obviously I was wrong.'

Tamsyn felt terrible, and for the first time she be-

146

came aware of her state of *déshabille*. Until then she had not considered that she was wearing only the cream silk wrapper she had worn from the bathroom to her bedroom.

'I—I'm sorry, Hywel,' she apologised awkwardly. 'I —I didn't think.'

'No.' He sounded remote. 'Now I suggest you do as I ask and get dressed. The Edwardses won't be in bed with this storm going on.'

Tamsyn sighed, and turning away she entered the sitting room switching on the light. 'I'm not leaving,' she said firmly. 'I don't want to go there. Can't you just accept that?'

Hywel came to the doorway, his hands in the pockets of his opened coat, disturbingly male and to her wonderfully familiar. 'I can't leave you here alone without even telephone communication to the outside world,' he insisted grimly. 'I'd never forgive myself——' He broke off abruptly. 'Tamsyn, won't you just be reasonable?'

Tamsyn regarded him regretfully. 'I'm not leaving,' she said again. 'But you can stay here, if you want to.'

Hywel's eyes hardened. 'You can't be serious!'

'Why not? There's plenty of room.'

Hywel turned away, resting his head against the door jamb, his forehead against his hand. 'Tamsyn, you know I can't stay here.'

Tamsyn grew impatient. Impatient with herself for allowing him to disturb her so, and impatient with him for not seeing the helplessness of her position.

'Why not?' she demanded, half tauntingly. 'Are you afraid to trust yourself?'

Hywel looked at her then and there was a tormented agony in his eyes, but his voice was bitter and cold. 'No, Tamsyn,' he said. 'I'm not an animal! I can control my instincts! It was you again that I was thinking of.'

Tamsyn felt the familiar sense of inadequacy assail her. 'Obviously I'm not good enough for you,' she said tremulously. 'My emotions are not so clinically controlled.' She squared her shoulders. 'If you'll excuse me, I think I'll go to bed. I'm rather tired.'

Hywel heaved a sigh. 'All right,' he said slowly. 'I'll stay. Where shall I sleep? Down here?'

Tamsyn shook her head jerkily. 'The couch would scarcely be big enough,' she said, crossing the room on shaking legs. 'You can use my bed. I'll sleep in my father's.'

Hywel stepped aside and she passed him with eyes averted. Upstairs, it was a tantalisingly disturbing experience showing him where her room was. But Hywel deliberately avoided looking at her and with a brief 'Goodnight' she left him and went into the master bedroom.

All the same, there was something reassuring about knowing he was within calling distance, and although she had not expected to sleep for hours, she didn't know another thing until the brilliant sunlight was probing her eyelids.

She got up lazily, peering out of her window on to the rain-washed fields. Everything smelt fresh and clean this morning and a sense of well-being enveloped her.

She dressed quickly in jeans and a cotton sweater, combing her hair and leaving it loose. Then she went downstairs and put on the kettle. There was no sign of Hywel and she went to the bottom of the stairs and looked up thoughtfully.

When the tea was made she put the teapot and two cups on a tray and carried them upstairs, going to her room in eager anticipation. But when she opened the door she found to her surprise that it was empty. Hywel had gone, and had it not been for the crumpled state of the bed she might have been inclined to believe she had dreamt the whole thing....

CHAPTER NINE

LANCE STANFORD arrived home soon after nine and seemed surprised to find Tamsyn there.

'I thought you'd still be up at Llanelfed,' he exclaimed.

Tamsyn coloured. 'I didn't go to Llanelfed, Daddy,' she explained carefully. 'I wouldn't go. I wanted to stay here.'

'You mean you stayed here alone—in all that storm?' Lance was horrified.

Tamsyn flushed more deeply. 'I—yes—why not?'

Her father shook his head. 'I told Hywel——'

'Yes, I know what you told Hywel, but I wouldn't go. Don't fuss, Daddy. I'm all right, really I am. Now, how's Joanna? And the baby?'

For the next half hour her father was diverted and told her all about his new son. They were going to call him Glyn, after Joanna's father who had died some few years ago.

'Glyn Stanford,' said Tamsyn experimentally. 'Yes, I like it.'

During the next few days Tamsyn saw little of her father. He spent his days between his patients and the hospital, only coming home to sleep, and Tamsyn used the time to get the house beautifully clean for Joanna's return.

But the day before Joanna was due to come home Tamsyn received a telegram, and after she had read it she cried for almost an hour. Not that it was bad news exactly. But when her father read it, he saw what it meant.

'She expects you to return to Boston at once,' he said. She noticed he did not say 'return home'.

'Yes.' Tamsyn felt almost physically sick.

'It says your mother has broken her ankle. Why can't anyone else take care of her until your holiday is over?'

Tamsyn sighed. 'Rebecca, Mummy's maid and house-keeper, is away in New Orleans, staying with her sister. I expect, as Charles has had to continue with the lecture tour, she's feeling pretty lonely on her own.'

Lance heaved a sigh. 'And what about me?' he demanded.

Tamsyn looked at him gently. 'Oh, Daddy, I don't want to go. But you have at least got Joanna—and your son!'

'I want my daughter, too,' he muttered grimly. 'Tamsyn, if I let you go, will you come back again?'

Tamsyn swallowed hard. 'I—I shall try.'

Lance nodded. 'Oh, well, there's nothing more I can say. Have—have you rung the airport? Made any arrangements yet?'

'No.' Tamsyn shook her head.

Lance sighed. 'And Joanna is coming home tomorrow. I know she was hoping you'd be here to help out with things.'

'And I wanted to be,' exclaimed Tamsyn passionately. 'But what can I do? She is my mother, and she expects me to go.'

'I know.' Lance rubbed the back of his neck wearily. 'All right, Tamsyn. I'll have a word with Hywel. If you can get a flight for tomorrow evening, maybe he would take you up to London.'

Tamsyn nodded eagerly, her heart lifting a little. Maybe on that long journey to town she would be able to persuade him to see things differently. Convince him that she would come back if he asked her to.

But in the event, it was not Hywel who took her to London, but David. When her father returned that afternoon it was to tell her with some surprise that Hywel had gone away a few days ago and Mrs. Williams didn't know where. This news was almost too much for Tamsyn to bear. That she should be leaving was bad enough. That she should be leaving without seeing Hywel was agonising.

On Thursday evening she went with her father to the hospital to see Joanna and the new baby and to say goodbye. Joanna was upset that she was leaving, too, and it was all Tamsyn could do to prevent herself crying right there in the maternity ward. She had been able to get a reservation on a flight from Heathrow leaving at seven o'clock the following evening, and this was to be her last night with her father. They sat up until the early hours talking, and by the time Tamsyn went to bed her father had assured himself that she would return just as soon as she possibly could.

David himself was rather remote on the journey to London. He sensed that Tamsyn's tearful departure from her father was not all that was troubling her, but he did not question her about it, for which she was thankful. She could not have borne an argument with him.

He didn't stay for the take-off making some excuse about it being a long way back to Trefallath. Tamsyn didn't really mind, but she felt very much alone as she walked the catwalk to the powerful Boeing.

Tamsyn dropped ice into the bucket with the tongs and then thrust the container back into the freezer.

Wiping her hands, she listened to the steady hum of voices from the lounge. The party was going well and her mother was enjoying being the centre of attraction again, elegantly relaxed on the chaise-longue. Everyone was commiserating with her for having broken her ankle, and having to leave her husband after only a few weeks of marriage to return home alone. But, they went on, she was lucky to have Tamsyn around to help her. What a wonderful daughter she must be to come home early from her own holiday to take care of her mother.

Tamsyn's lips twisted. In the last week since her return she had heard it all, all the old clichés about loyalty and daughterly duty. What would they think, she wondered, if she were to tell them how she really felt? What would be their reaction to her announcement that she had only come home because Laura had practically insisted that she should do so? That she had not wanted to come back to Boston at all? That she continually fought the feeling of resentment that engulfed her when she considered the curtailment of her own arrangements? How could they be expected to understand how despairing was the frustration she managed outwardly to suppress?

Since returning to Boston she had written to her father, but she had had no reply as yet, and she ached for news of Hywel. She would have liked to have written to him, too, but until she knew that he had returned to Trefallath she would not risk the letter falling into Mrs. Williams's hands.

During the long nights that she had lain awake since her return she had come to a decision. When her mother was sufficiently recovered to listen she was going to suggest that once Charles returned from his lecture tour she might return to Wales. She didn't know quite how she was going to phrase such a request; her mother would be sure to question the advisability of neglecting her studies apart from anything else; but somehow it had to be made clear that Tamsyn considered herself old enough to make such decisions for herself.

And after all, now that her mother was married again, Tamsyn's position in the household became much less important. Already her mother had taken to discussing her work with Charles in much the same way as she had once discussed it with Tamsyn, and besides, it was what Tamsyn herself wanted to do.

Even so, the prospect was daunting to say the least, and although they had spoken about Lance and Joanna, and the new baby, since Tamsyn's return, never at any time had it been assumed that Tamsyn had spent anything more than a rather obligatory sojourn with her father. Laura seemed to regard the fact of Lance's having a child as somewhat distasteful, and Tamsyn realised, with a self-recriminatory flash of remembrance, that that was exactly how she had reacted in the beginning.

But it was different for her. Her ties with her father were as strong as they ever were, while Laura had cut the silver cord for good. Tamsyn wondered if she never regretted giving up the love of a man like her father for the much less attractive demands of a career. Although Tamsyn herself had always imagined that that was what she wanted, too, during recent weeks she had come to know herself so much better. Hywel had been right when he had told her that her weeks in the valley would teach her a lot. Only he had not then been aware that he was to play an integral part in that education.

The following week there was a letter from her father. Tamsyn picked it up from the doormat when she went downstairs one morning to prepare Laura's breakfast tray. Laura had taken to having breakfast in bed, and usually Tamsyn appreciated these few minutes alone before she had to respond to her mother's somewhat demanding personality.

Carrying the letter into the kitchen, a streamlined, space-age type kitchen, that bore no resemblance to Joanna's scrubbed cleanliness or Hywel's untidy cooking area, she perched on a stool at the breakfast bar and slit open the envelope.

Scanning the pages that emerged, she felt herself temporarily transported back to the valley, to her father's house in its fold of moorland. First of all he thanked her for her letter, telling her how delighted he had been to receive it and to know that once out of sight he was not out of Tamsyn's mind. Then he went on about Joanna's return from hospital and how much weight Glyn was gaining. The baby was to be christened in six weeks' time and he suggested tentatively that she might come back for the event.

Tamsyn read on urgently, a warmth developing inside her as Lance went on to describe how much they all missed her. Joanna said the house was empty without her.

He touched briefly on what they had discussed the night before she came away, and urged her to consider making Trefallath her second home.

Tamsyn came to the end with misgivings. It had been wonderful to hear from her father, to know that he was thinking about her, but there had been no mention of Hywel. Why? Was he still away? Or did her father not consider it important to mention him? And why should he, after all? So far as he was concerned, Hywel meant no more to her than David Edwards, and he hadn't mentioned him either.

Folding the letter back into its envelope, Tamsyn slid off the stool and went to plug in the percolator. She might as well accept the fact that so far as Hywel was concerned her return to the States was the inevitable end of a rather untidy episode. He considered the affair closed, and so should she. Apart from all the other issues, he was married, and obviously had no intention of changing that situation.

The days that followed the arrival of her father's letter seemed harder to bear somehow than those earlier days. She was torn between the desire to tell her mother that she wanted to return to Wales, and the crushing humiliation she would feel if Hywel again refused to regard their relationship seriously.

Gerry Thorpe returned to Boston a couple of days later. Because of Tamsyn's break-up of their holiday plans, he had accompanied his parents to Miami Beach for a prolonged vacation, and he was delighted to find that Tamsyn was already home.

He came round the night he returned and at her mother's suggestion he took Tamsyn for a drive in his father's car. In truth Tamsyn was aware that her mother was becoming increasingly concerned about her, realising as the days went by that although her daughter appeared to be exactly the same as before she went away, beneath the surface she had changed. Laura was unable to put her finger on any specific thing or she would have brought it up with her, but nevertheless she welcomed the return of Gerry Thorpe as another step towards the kind of situation that had existed before Tamsyn went away.

Gerry was reassuringly unchanged. They drove out to the Sound and sat in the car, talking and exchanging experiences.

'So how was Wales?' he asked, lighting a cigarette. 'And your father? Was it as bad as you expected?'

'It wasn't bad at all,' replied Tamsyn shortly. 'I—I had a marvellous time!'

'I bet.'

'I did, too. Daddy was very kind, and Joanna wasn't at all like I expected her to be.'

Gerry sighed. 'Then how come you came back so smartly?'

'Mummy broke her ankle.'

'So?'

'So she needed me. Charles continued with the lecture tour, you see.'

'So what? Surely your mother could have gotten herself a nurse! You needn't have come haring back here to play the devoted daughter.'

Tamsyn hunched her shoulders. 'Oh, you know Mummy. She wanted me. So I came.'

Gerry nodded. 'Yeah, I know Mummy,' he said dryly.

Tamsyn sighed. 'So what did you do? Was Miami Beach fun?'

'Oh, yes, it was great! The only time I wore a shirt was in the evenings.'

Tamsyn smiled. 'You are tanned.'

'So are you. I guess this climate in England wasn't so bad after all.'

'Wales,' corrected Tamsyn, playing with the tendrils of hair that brushed her cheek. 'And no, the weather was pretty good.'

'What did you do?'

'Do?' Tamsyn shrugged. 'Oh, well, I sunbathed, and I helped Joanna about the house——'

'Some holiday!'

'I didn't mind. She—she was expecting a baby when I arrived. She had it a week before I came away.'

'A baby!' Gerry raised his eyebrows. 'Gosh, I thought—well, I mean—didn't you mind?'

Tamsyn considered. 'I did at first. But then I realised how silly it was—minding something like that. I mean, they love one another, and it's the most natural thing in the world, after all.'

'I guess so.' Gerry regarded her intently. 'Gee, Tamsyn, I missed you.'

'Did you?' Tamsyn couldn't meet his eyes. 'That's nice.'

'I gather from that rather insipid little comment that you didn't miss me!' he remarked, rubbing his ear.

Tamsyn made a helpless gesture. 'I—I didn't say that——'

'You didn't have to. It's obvious. It's okay, Tamsyn. I've known all along I was nothing special so far as you're concerned.'

'Oh, Gerry!'

'It's my own fault. I knew it wasn't as important to you as it is. to me when you refused to go against your mother and come away with me.'

'I like you, Gerry.'

Gerry nodded. 'Fine.' Determinedly he changed the subject. 'They're having a sort of tennis tournament over at the McQueens' on Tuesday afternoon. How about coming on over with me?'

Tamsyn hesitated, and then she relaxed. 'Why not?'

she agreed. 'It might be fun.'

By the time Charles returned, full of confidence from his lecture tour, and Tamsyn had summoned up enough courage to approach her mother about returning to Wales, Laura had convinced herself that she had been mistaken in thinking her daughter had changed. In recent weeks, she had been out almost every day with Gerry Thorpe, or with one or other of the young group they mixed with, and it seemed that her trip to Europe and the visit with her father were past and forgotten.

So it was with shocked surprise that Laura, newly liberated from her plaster, listened to Tamsyn asking whether she might speak to her privately one evening.

With a twinge of alarm feathering along her veins, Laura frowned impatiently. 'We are private, darling. Whatever you have to say you can say in front of Charles.'

Charles was seated comfortably in his armchair after dinner, reading a newspaper, a glass of brandy beside him. The autumn semester was about to begin and both he and her mother were making the most of these last few days before their work commandeered their time.

Tamsyn hesitated and then gave a resigned sigh. 'Very well. I want you to allow me to return to Trefallath.'

Laura could not have looked more stunned, and even Charles folded his newspaper and stared at her.

'You mean—you mean—go back to your father?' asked Laura faintly.

'Yes. For a time.'

'What do you mean—for a time?'

'I—I thought perhaps six months——'

'*Six months!*' Laura was horrified. 'But what about your studies?'

Tamsyn expelled her breath jerkily. 'They could wait.'

Charles got up from his chair. 'Don't you think you're behaving rather foolishly?' he asked. 'Is this your father's suggestion?'

'No. It's mine.' Tamsyn resented having to answer to Charles like this. He was not related to her. She felt more affinity with Joanna than with him, for all she had known him so much longer.

'But I don't understand.' Laura fanned herself with her handkerchief. 'Whatever are you going to do at Trefallath for six months?'

Tamsyn shrugged. 'Exactly the same as I should do here, I suppose.'

'But you wouldn't be able to continue your studies!' repeated Laura.

'I know. Strange as it may seem, Mummy, people can get along without that sort of thing.'

'Oh, this is all your father's doing!' exclaimed Laura, losing patience. 'I knew I shouldn't have let you go.'

'That's not true!' Tamsyn was indignant. 'He hasn't tried to persuade me, one way or the other. It's my own decision. I want to go back.'

'I don't understand, I simply don't understand.' Laura rose from her seat on the chaise-longue and limped across to pour herself a glass of sherry. 'I always thought you were happy here.'

'I was—I *am*!' Tamsyn made a frustrated gesture. 'Mummy, people can be happy in different ways.'

'But you've never wanted to do anything like this before.'

160

'I didn't know my father before!' retorted Tamsyn.

'Precisely,' said Charles heavily. 'It's obvious, whatever protestations you might make, that this all hinges on him!'

'It doesn't!' declared Tamsyn passionately. 'He's only part of it.'

Laura's brows drew together. 'And what is that supposed to mean?' she demanded icily.

Tamsyn pressed her palms together. 'Well—well, there's someone else.'

'Someone else?' Laura stared at her. 'What do you mean?'

'I mean there's someone else I want to see again.'

Laura raised her eyes heavenward. 'Oh, God! Not some unrequited teenage crush!'

'It's nothing like that!' cried Tamsyn, her cheeks burning.

'Then what is it like? Good heavens, Tamsyn, aren't there enough young men here for you to take your pick? Did you have to go and get involved with some pimply-faced youth fresh from the coal-face!'

'That's—that's unforgivable!' Tamsyn was horrified.

Charles raised a hand calmingly. 'Now don't let's get hysterical about this,' he advised carefully. 'Allowing this discussion to deteriorate into a slanging match is not going to help anyone. I suggest we allow Tamsyn to tell us what she means quietly and calmly.'

Laura pressed her handkerchief to her lips. 'I don't want to hear. It's ludicrous!'

Charles gave her a hard look and she subsided on to the couch, blowing her nose vigorously. Then he turned to Tamsyn.

'Now,' he said, 'what is this all about?'

Tamsyn moved her shoulders a trifle nervously. 'It's

quite simple really. I've fallen in love.'

'Oh, spare me that, at least,' moaned Laura bitterly.

'It's true!' cried Tamsyn urgently. 'I can't help it. I didn't want it to happen—I didn't expect it to happen, but it did.'

'And who is this young man?' asked Charles, ignoring his wife's distress for the moment. 'Where does he live? What does he do?'

Tamsyn swallowed with difficulty. 'He—he's not a young man, exactly,' she said carefully.

Laura pricked up her ears. 'What do you mean? Who is he?'

'He—he's a friend of Daddy's,' said Tamsyn quickly. 'A writer. And he lives in the village.'

'A writer!' snapped Laura disbelievingly. 'What does he write?'

'Give her time,' said Charles impatiently.

'He writes novels,' went on Tamsyn reluctantly. 'His name is Hywel Benedict.'

'*Hywel Benedict!*' Laura was flabbergasted. 'Hywel Benedict! Good God, Tamsyn, you're not involved with him!'

'I didn't say I was involved with him,' Tamsyn exclaimed quickly. 'Mummy, it's not like that.'

'What is all this?' Charles was confused now. 'Do you know this man, Laura?'

'Know him? Know him? Of course I know him. Joanna is his cousin. Why, he even attended our wedding, Lance's and mine.'

Charles looked perplexed. 'And this is the man you're in love with, Tamsyn?'

'Yes.' Tamsyn ignored Laura's gasp of derision.

'And he's in love with you?'

Tamsyn bent her head. 'No, I didn't say that,' she

replied quietly. 'He—he regards me as a child.'

'I should think he does!' Laura was somewhat mollified by Tamsyn's answer. 'Heavens, Charles, the idea's ridiculous!'

Tamsyn looked up then. 'Why is it ridiculous?'

Laura gave her an exasperated stare. 'Because the man's too old for you, of course. And in any case, he's unsuitable.'

'To whom?' persisted Tamsyn relentlessly.

'To you—to me—to everyone! Tamsyn, I've been very patient with you, but I don't want to hear any more about it.'

'Laura!' That was Charles's voice holding a faint warning. 'Laura, don't be too hasty.'

'Why? Why shouldn't I be hasty?'

Charles frowned. 'Well, because Tamsyn is not a child, of course, no matter how she may appear to you. She'll be eighteen next month. Old enough to make decisions for herself.'

Laura opened her mouth to protest again, and then closed it. She always listened to Charles's advice, weighing it, valuing it. She understood what he was trying to get across to her and his quiet words prevented her from spilling out the bitterness and resentment that trembled on her tongue.

Controlling herself, she said, with obvious reluctance: 'Well, Charles? What is your opinion?'

Charles tugged thoughtfully at his chin. 'I think we should seriously consider letting her go, if that's what she wants to do,' he said, shocking his wife into silence. 'But not yet.'

Tamsyn, who had thought she had found an unexpected ally, turned to him uncertainly. 'Not yet?' she echoed. 'What do you mean?'

163

Charles ran his tongue over his soft lips. 'Well, I suggest we leave it for the present, but if you feel the same at Christmas we'll discuss it again—how about that?'

Tamsyn stared at him. Christmas was almost four months away. And yet . . .

'And if I do?' she asked.

'Then we'd have to let you go, of course.' He turned to his wife. 'Wouldn't we, Laura?'

Laura moved restlessly, almost shredding her handkerchief between her nervous fingers. 'If—if you say so, Charles,' she agreed reluctantly.

Charles folded his hands behind his back. 'I think it's the fairest assessment of the situation,' he stated pedantically. 'And after all, Tamsyn, you mean everything to your mother, you know that. You wouldn't really want to do something against which she was wholly opposed, would you?'

'Well—no.' Tamsyn felt slightly discomfited.

'Good. It's settled then.' Charles managed a faint smile. 'And now I suggest we forget all about it. Is Gerry coming over this evening?'

Tamsyn felt frustration knotting inside her. No matter what Charles said, she didn't altogether trust him. How could he agree to her going to Wales one moment, and the next ask whether she was about to go out with Gerry Thorpe? The two things were incompatible. Hadn't he listened to what she had said about Hywel? Didn't her protestations mean anything to him?

She turned to her mother. Laura was sipping sherry weakly, casting reproachful glances in Tamsyn's direction, expecting her to apologise for the scene that had just taken place.

Tamsyn was tempted to rail at them, at both of them. She was tempted to tell them that she intended to do exactly as she liked; that she would go to Wales and marry Hywel, or just live with him if he would have her! That no matter what they said or however long they made her wait, sooner or later she would go back.

CHAPTER TEN

TAMSYN wrote and told her father that she would not be able to return to Trefallath in time for Glyn's christening. She hated disappointing him like this, but she eagerly went on to tell him that she had spoken to her mother about spending some time in Wales and she hoped to see them all again soon after Christmas. It was a rather unsatisfactory promise, and she hoped her father would understand what she was trying to convey.

Writing to Hywel was much more difficult. To begin with, she couldn't be sure he was back home again, and no matter how she tried she could not get the words to sound right. When she poured out her true feelings on to paper they looked wildly romantic, the foolish garblings of a love-struck adolescent, which was the last thing she wanted him to think. But when she tried to control these same feelings and merely write the kind of letter one would send to a friend it looked cold and stilted, filled with the details of her activities, reflecting the superficial kind of life she was leading.

Eventually she had to give it up, and she waited desperately to see whether he might write to her. In the letter she had sent to her father she had asked about Hywel, how he was, whether he was back, and so on, and she prayed he might hear of this and decide to write himself.

But the days and weeks went by without further word from either of them, and Tamsyn, immersed in the academic life of the college, tried to concentrate all her energies in other directions. It was useless looking forward to Christmas. The festival was a nebulous goal at best and the aching knowledge that Hywel had let her leave without making any small attempt to get in touch with her gnawed at her like a disease. To consider going back there to face his indifference was a gruelling prospect. And yet she knew that no matter how ignominious might be her defeat she must try again.

There were times when she asked herself why she should feel so sure about her feelings. What was there about Hywel that attracted her? Among her friends here in Boston there were young men, tall, broad, handsome young men, who were quite prepared to make her forget the past had she allowed them to do so. And yet she felt no response towards them. Why? If what she felt for Hywel was merely a physical, sexual urgency, why couldn't some other man fill the aching void?

It was at times like these that she felt almost desperate. She *loved* Hywel, that was the difference. He was the only man she wanted. And if she couldn't have him she would have no one. All she asked was the chance to live near him, to see him now and then. Her love was enough.

Her mother and Charles, she knew, were hoping that the prolonged separation would achieve what all their arguments would not. Once Tamsyn overheard them speaking together and although she knew she ought not to listen the mention of her and Hywel's names was sufficient to rivet her to the spot. It confirmed her earlier suspicions of Charles at any rate. His apparent falling-in with her plans had merely been a ploy to give them time to persuade her that her life was here in Boston, with them.

And they might have succeeded, Tamsyn admitted to herself honestly, had her feelings for Hywel been the illusory emotions they imagined them to be. After all, materially she had everything any girl could wish for. On her eighteenth birthday in October, Laura presented her with a small sports car, and although Tamsyn accepted that this was part of their plan for keeping her there, she couldn't fail to find it exciting having her own transport.

Gerry taught her to drive and by the time the first flakes of snow began to fall she was as proficient as he. She appreciated Gerry's companionship during those weeks. Aware that he held no especial place in her thoughts, he proved himself a good friend, and although Tamsyn knew her mother would have chosen someone more aggressively masculine for her Tamsyn preferred Gerry's uncomplicated company.

Christmas was getting nearer and suddenly Tamsyn began to feel excited. The weeks and months between had gradually slipped by and soon she would have to hold her mother and Charles to their promise. She had told Gerry she was going back to Wales after Christmas and he had been amazed.

'What on earth do you want to do that for?' he had asked. Then with narrowed eyes, 'Are you sure there's not some guy there you haven't told me about?'

Tamsyn had made some evasive reply, but she sensed that Gerry didn't altogether believe her. Not that she minded really. Sooner or later he would get to know, one way or the other.

Christmas Day was quite pleasant. The Penmans gave a party in the evening and several of Tamsyn's friends were invited along with their parents. There were games and kisses under the mistletoe and the giving and receiving of presents, and Tamsyn forced herself not to speculate on Hywel's Christmas, possibly alone in his house beside the chapel, eating some terrible fare that Mrs. Williams had prepared for him.

The day after Christmas, Boxing Day, Laura developed a virus infection.

At first Tamsyn was very sympathetic. Laura was confined to her bedroom and did look terribly frail after her frequent attacks of vomiting. Tamsyn helped Rebecca as much as she could, winning Charles's approval, and generally creating a comfortable atmosphere. But as the days went by and Laura improved things changed.

It became obvious that Laura's prolonged sojourn in bed was not wholly designed to improve her health. So long as she remained upstairs, apart from the rest of the household, Tamsyn could not very well trouble her with her affairs, and the New Year came in without anything further being said about Tamsyn leaving Boston.

One afternoon Tamsyn did try to bring up the subject with Charles, but his reaction was to shake his head and tell her that she would have to wait until her mother was well again.

Frustration set in and Tamsyn paced her room like a caged lion. She had done what they asked. She had waited until Christmas. Why couldn't they let her go as they had promised?

Eventually she came to a decision. She would go and not tell them. She had sufficient money to cover her fare, her passport was valid; what more did she need? She would send her mother a cablegram from the airport explaining where she had gone, and Laura could send her clothes on to her. So long as she had a few things with her—she wouldn't need a lot.

She considered cabling her father that she was coming, but then changed her mind. He might urge her to tell her mother what she was planning to do and she could not risk that, not in the circumstances.

It was incredibly easy making her arrangements. Having her own car meant she did not have to make excuses as to where she was going, and so long as she appeared to be having a good time, both Charles and her mother made no demur.

Smuggling her case out of the house seemed the hardest thing to achieve, particularly as Rebecca always seemed to appear in the hall at the most inopportune moments. But Tamsyn took it out the evening before she left under cover of darkness and locked it in the trunk of her car without anyone observing her activities.

Her flight was scheduled to leave at noon Boston time and although Laura was still pretending to be confined to her bedroom, Tamsyn felt obliged to spend part of the morning with her.

However, Laura was not at all enthusiastic about spending so much time with her daughter. No doubt she was afraid there might be an opportunity to discuss what was uppermost in both their minds, thought Tamsyn cynically, as Laura assumed a weary expression and politely suggested that Tamsyn should leave her alone to rest.

Tamsyn left without misgivings. The cord that had bound her to Laura was severed and nothing either of them could do would alter that.

She arrived at the airport much too early, checking

in and then spending several impatient minutes kicking her heels in the lounge. She was eager to get away before someone recognised her. The airport was a busy meeting place and at this time of the year, with people returning from visits to relatives and such like for the festive season, there was every possibility of someone she knew running into her.

When her name was paged over the loudspeaker system some few minutes later, she felt her heart skip a beat, convinced that somehow or other Laura had discovered her plans. A desire to run, to escape from what seemed to be the inevitable overwhelmed her, but then common sense took over again and she walked dully towards the desk.

The receptionist smiled politely. 'Miss Stanford?' she questioned, and at Tamsyn's nod went on: 'I'm afraid your flight has been delayed, Miss Stanford. There's some problem with the fuel consumption, and it might be several hours before take-off.'

Tamsyn's spirits, which had risen at her first words, plummeted. 'Damn!' she exclaimed. 'Is there nothing you can do?'

The girl hesitated. 'There's a flight leaving for New York in a few minutes, Miss Stanford. I can book you on to that, and you'd pick up a definite connection from there soon after—let me see—three o'clock? That's the best I can suggest, I'm afraid.'

'Oh, that's fine!' Tamsyn was eager. In New York no one would recognise her. 'What do I do?'

While the receptionist dealt with the details, Tamsyn hurriedly approached the telegraph office and wrote out her cable to her mother. Then it was time to board the flight to New York, and she took her seat rather apprehensively, her nerves jumping with excitement. She could hardly believe she was actually on her way at last.

It was dark by the time the trundling country bus reached Trefallath. Tamsyn had not known there was a bus service she could use until now, but she was grateful for any means of transport to reach her destination. Altogether it had been a rather tiring journey from London and her bones ached from constantly being confined to a sitting position.

The massive jumbo jet which had carried her from New York to London had landed in the early hours of the morning, and Tamsyn had managed to get a taxi into London and book in at a hotel. Her warm smile and attractive appearance opened many doors for her and for once she was glad that she was young and good-looking.

This morning she had checked out of the hotel again after consultation with the receptionist, who had advised her to go to Paddington station and make further enquiries there about reaching Trefallath.

The station staff had been helpful, but she had to make several changes before reaching Llandrindod Wells, which was the nearest station to the valley.

It had been late afternoon by the time she reached Llandrindod Wells, but after making enquiries about buses and learning that one was leaving in fifteen minutes she had not stopped to get anything to eat but had boarded it immediately, realising from the state of the weather that there most probably would not be another that night. Ever since leaving London, there had been increasing evidence of previous falls of snow, and although it was not snowing at the moment, the wind was like a knife, and it was freezing hard.

The bus dropped her just outside the village about a quarter of a mile from her father's house. Tamsyn felt the icy wind tear down the valley, as the bus rolled away, thrusting its probing fingers into the warmth of her sheepskin coat. Beneath the warm thigh-length jacket she was wearing a navy blue trouser suit that was thankfully thick and close-fitting, but in spite of that she was unused to the chilling blast of a wind in open country.

Thrusting down the hollow feeling of emptiness that made her feel slightly nauseated, she began to walk briskly up the road to her father's house. What did it matter what the weather was like? She was here at last, and maybe tomorrow she would see Hywel again.

But when she reached her father's house she found it was in darkness, and her heart sank. She trailed round the back, her arm aching a little from carrying her case so far, but there was no sign of life.

Stamping her feet in an effort to keep them warm, she looked about her uncertainly. The very last thing she had expected was for them to be out. But perhaps they were not just out, a small voice suggested. Perhaps they were away for a few days. Surely no one would take a baby out at this time of night unless they intended staying overnight somewhere.

A nagging anxiety that this might be so tugged at her. She ought to have telegraphed her father, after all. He ought to have been forewarned of her coming. No one in their right minds would just pack up and leave to visit someone more than three thousand miles away without first warning them that they were coming. She was a fool! And what was she going to do now?

Sighing, she looked down at her toes. There was

only one thing to do. She would have to go and throw herself on Hywel's generosity. And what if he refused to take her in? What then?

She refused to admit to the feeling of panic that assailed her, and with quickening steps she hastened off down the road towards the village again. A few flakes of snow began to fall, blowing into her face and resting on her long lashes. She brushed them away impatiently. It was so cold! If only it wcre not so bitterly cold!

The village was deserted except for the sound of a few voices coming from the open door of the pub. Her heart rose a little. Perhaps she could get lodging there if Hywel refused her his hospitality. Maybe she should go there first—but her confidence ebbed at this thought. To picture herself entering the bar of the Bull and requesting a bed for the night didn't bear thinking about. She could imagine the kind of gossip that would arouse.

Hywel's house was unlighted, too, and the awful feeling of panic she had crushed earlier came back to taunt her. What was she going to do now? It looked as though it would have to be the pub, after all.

On impulse, she opened Hywel's gate and walked up the path to his door. Summoning her courage, she knocked loudly on the panels and waited expectantly. But nothing happened. There was no sound from inside, and her spirits sank. Pressing her lips together, she took hold of the door handle and rattled impatiently, and to her surprise the door opened inwards.

She gasped and stood back looking into the dark well of the hall. 'H—hello?' she called faintly, and then more vigorously: 'Hello! Is anybody there? Hywel?'

There was no reply and she looked round apprehensively, half afraid that her calls had attracted attention to herself, but there was no one around to hear her, and taking a deep breath she stepped inside.

With the front door closed, the hall was very dark, but she dared not put on the light there in case anyone saw it and wondered who was trespassing inside. So she felt her way along the passage to the living-room door and switched on the light.

Everywhere looked much the same as usual, except perhaps there was a more generous film of dust over everything. Obviously Mrs. Williams had given herself a holiday over Christmas and New Year and it didn't look as though she'd returned to work yet.

But for all that the room was beautifully warm. Before going out, wherever he was, Hywel had built up the fire, and although now it was reduced to a mass of glowing embers, there was plenty of coal in the hod beside the hearth to build it up again.

Tamsyn set to work and did just this, and when it was blazing merrily she went out into the kitchen. She was ravenous by this time, and she hoped he wouldn't mind if she made herself a cup of coffee and a sandwich. As she munched her way through a wedge of cheese and some reasonably new bread, which seemed to prove that Hywel couldn't be far away, she decided he must be at the pub. A glance at her watch told her that it would be closing time soon, and her nerves jerked uneasily. All of a sudden she was no longer hungry, and she thrust the remains of her sandwich into the waste bin and carried her coffee through to the living room.

But closing time came and went without Hywel's appearance, and Tamsyn, curled on the couch in front of the warm fire, began to feel drowsy. Where were they all? she asked herself wearily. Hywel, and her father, Joanna and the baby...

She must have slept, but she came awake with a start to the certain knowledge that someone was in the house. A prickle of unease crept along her nerves. She had not locked the front door, and anyone could have entered, just as she did.

The sounds came from upstairs, however, and she blinked rapidly, trying to distinguish the hands on the face of her watch. It was after one o'clock. It had to be Hywel! Had he already been in here and seen her? Did he think to leave her to sleep there as she appeared so comfortable?

But she was not so comfortable as she had been. The fire had died down again, and the room was beginning to feel distinctly chilly.

She got off the couch and went to the living-room door. The landing light revealed that whoever was upstairs was not afraid to be seen. She walked to the foot of the stairs and hesitated. If he didn't know she was here it was going to be a shock for him seeing her suddenly like this. Perhaps she should wait until he came downstairs again.

But perhaps he would not come down, an inner voice argued. What if he had come home and was going straight to bed? Her heart thumped heavily. What ought she to do? All of a sudden she was not sure of herself any more. She had not changed, but what about Hywel? Five months was a long time. Oh, if only her father had been at home! She could have gone there and her first meeting with Hywel would have been a natural one, not this unexpected and unwanted confrontation.

Slowly, she ascended the stairs, expecting every moment to be halted by his angry observation of her presence. But she gained the landing without incident and looked about her nervously. There was a light coming from one of the bedrooms and on uncertain feet she walked to the half-opened doorway.

Hywel was getting undressed. He had taken off his shirt and his back was bare to her. She could not let him go any further.

'Hywel!' she murmured tentatively. 'Hywel, I've been waiting for you!'

The violent way he turned to her, the look of consternation on his face, should have warned her that there was more to his agonised expression than mere surprise at her unexpected appearance. But she was too shocked by his appearance to pay much attention in those first few seconds to his reactions. The flesh had fallen off him and his muscular body was much thinner than she remembered. But his face was the most revealing. His eyes, which had always been deep-set, were sunken into his head and there was a haggard expression in their depths.

'*Tamsyn!*' he muttered disbelievingly, shaking his head. 'God, I'm having hallucinations now! Can't you leave me alone?'

The tormented vehemence of his rejection of her living presence made Tamsyn stare at him in desperation. 'You're not having hallucinations, Hywel,' she said quietly. 'It's really me! I've come back. Only it's obvious I'm not wanted.'

She turned stumblingly, conscious of only one need, that of putting sufficient distance between herself and Hywel to assuage the grinding pain of his rejection.

But he moved more swiftly than she and before she

could reach the stairs he had caught her, his hands
heavy on her slim shoulders, dragging her relentlessly
back against him. His hands slid over her possessively,
assuring himself of her reality, pressing her closer as
though to penetrate the flesh and blood woman she
was. Then he groaned and buried his face in the thick-
ness of the hair at the nape of her neck. 'Tamsyn,
Tamsyn, Tamsyn,' he breathed thickly. 'Oh, Tamsyn,
I can't believe it, I just can't believe it.'

Tamsyn's whole being was suffused with warmth
from his hard body. She closed her eyes, letting emotion engulf her, just wanting him to go on holding her
like this, *loving* her ... But when she would have
turned and sought his mouth, he drew back, shaking
his head a trifle dazedly.

'Dear God, Tamsyn,' he muttered. 'If I touch you
any more I won't be able to stop, and I've got to.'

'Why? Why must you always be so sane and sensible? Don't you want me?' She allowed the tips of her
fingers to move against the hair-roughened skin of his
chest.

Hywel caught her disturbingly sensuous fingers in
his hands, holding her grimly at arm's length. 'Tamsyn!' he said harshly. 'You don't understand——'

'That's right, I don't.' Tamsyn stared at him appealingly. 'Aren't you pleased to see me?'

Hywel moved his head slowly from side to side.
'Pleased?' he echoed weakly. 'God, you don't know
what seeing you means to me!'

'Then why——'

'Wait!' Hywel looked down at his half naked body.
'Look, I must put some clothes on! Go downstairs and
wait for me.'

'Can't I wait here?'

Hywel released her fingers and turned away. 'If you like,' he agreed huskily.

Tamsyn watched him go back into his bedroom, unable for the moment to think of anything but her love for him. Nothing had changed; Hywel still wanted her. And that was enough—for now.

Hywel returned wearing a thick cream sweater and indicated that she should precede him downstairs. In the dining room, when she would have gone into his arms again, he said: 'Tamsyn, be sensible for a minute! Don't you realise I thought you were *dead*!'

'Dead?' Tamsyn drew her brows together. 'But—but why should you think that?'

Hywel pressed her firmly down on to the couch again, and then he took up a position on the hearth, feet slightly apart, facing her. 'Now,' he said quietly, 'how did you get here?'

Tamsyn shrugged perplexedly. 'What do you mean? I got a bus from Llandrindod——'

Hywel sighed impatiently. 'I don't mean that, Tamsyn. I mean—how did you get from Boston to London?'

'Why—by plane, of course.'

Hywel clenched his fists, obviously under some kind of strain. 'Tamsyn, the plane you were scheduled to travel on crashed on to the runway seconds after take-off!'

Tamsyn stared at him for a long moment and then the colour slowly drained out of her cheeks. 'Oh, God!' she breathed, and he nodded.

'Now do you understand why I was so stunned to see you? I've just come back from London Airport with your father. He's in a terrible state, but no worse than your mother, believe me! When she telephoned the news yesterday evening——' He broke off abruptly. 'We all thought you were dead! We've been trying to make enquiries, but there's been so much confusion at both ends——'

'Were—were there any survivors?' whispered Tamsyn weakly.

'About half a dozen, I think. As I say, everything's been chaotic. All that's emerged today is that you definitely were not one of them.' He took a long shaking breath. 'I must let your father know. He's been out of his mind with worry!'

'Yes! Yes, of course.' Tamsyn got to her feet, grasping his strong arm with both hands, shock and awareness sweeping over her in equal amounts. 'Hywel, hold me—hold me a minute! I feel sick!'

Hywel gathered her closely against him and then, as always when their bodies touched, desire stirred between them, overcoming all other emotions. With a muffled exclamation, Hywel cupped her throat in his hands, turning her face up to his with his thumbs, his mouth seeking the parted urgency of hers.

Tamsyn trembled. There was a hungry need in his kiss that only complete surrender would satisfy, and the way he was holding her against him sent her senses spinning with the knowledge of that need.

'I love you, I love you,' he muttered in a tortured voice. 'I want you! You don't know what it's been like —these last few hours have been hell——'

'I do know,' she protested huskily. 'Hywel, why did you go away like that? Why didn't you write to me? I've missed you so——'

Hywel's mouth moved against hers, exploring, deepening, druggingly creating that wonderful lethargy inside her. 'How could I write?' he demanded violently. 'I went away to think and when I came back you were gone! Tamsyn, I've got nothing to offer a girl like you——'

'Only yourself,' she breathed, sliding her hands beneath his sweater, next to his warm skin. 'I don't want anything else but you!'

'If I could believe that——' he groaned, and then with an immense effort he dragged himself away from her. 'Tamsyn, this won't do! I must put your father out of his misery! And he'll want to book a call to Boston as well. For your mother's sake.'

'Oh, yes, Mummy!' Tamsyn bent her head. 'She'll be frantic! But how was I to know—to guess that that plane——' She broke off. 'When I got to the airport I was told they were having some trouble with my flight, so—so I flew to New York and picked up a connection from there.'

'Thank God you did!' Hywel's face was pale. 'Without the telegram you sent your mother, none of us would have known...' He shook his head. 'She said you'd run away.'

Tamsyn sighed. 'Hardly that,' she murmured wryly. 'I was merely showing her and Charles that they could no longer rule my life for me.' She looked up, her lips tremulous. 'Hywel, after you've made this call—after you've told Daddy—what then?'

Hywel shook his head, making a supreme effort to control his instincts which were all sensuous at the moment. 'I—don't—know,' he ground out helplessly. He raked a hand through his hair. 'Just let me make the call!'

The next few minutes were very emotional ones for Tamsyn. Her father was so relieved to hear her voice again and to know that she was alive and well that he broke down completely. Hywel himself had to take the phone from Tamsyn's trembling fingers and promise that he would drive Tamsyn up to her father's house immediately. It was the only thing to do.

Tamsyn waited until he had replaced the receiver and then she said: 'I'd better get my things, hadn't I?'

Hywel nodded without looking at her, reaching for his coat.

With reluctant steps Tamsyn went back into the living room and pulled on her sheepskin jacket. Her hair was in disorder, but she didn't particularly care. She dreaded leaving this house to come back tomorrow to Hywel's enforced indifference.

When she emerged into the hall with her suitcase he was buttoning his coat, and she stood the case down uncertainly, looking at him appealingly.

'Hywel,' she whispered weakly. 'What—what you said just now—about—about having nothing to offer me—did—did you mean it?'

Hywel looked at her then, and she thought again how lean he was to what he had been. 'Yes, I meant it!' he replied abruptly, unable in this moment of truth to lie to her.

Tamsyn's heart lifted. 'Then—then you're not married any more?'

Hywel thrust his hands deep into his coat pockets. 'I was never married,' he replied harshly. 'When Maureen married me, she was already married to some chap she met in London years before. It was only when he came looking for her that I found out. She left with him.'

Tamsyn's lips parted. 'Oh, Hywel, why didn't you

tell me this before? Why did you let me go on thinking you were married?'

Hywel turned away. 'Because it was easier that way,' he muttered roughly. 'Tamsyn, I'm too old for you! It was easier holding you off when you thought I was a married man.'

Tamsyn quivered. 'And now?'

'Now—I don't know.' He shrugged. 'An hour ago, I thought, because you were dead, that my life was over. But knowing you're safe ... To take what you're offering—to ruin your life——'

Tamsyn went round to face him angrily. 'How can you say that?' she demanded. 'Are you sure it's not just an excuse because Maureen ruined yours?'

Hywel shook his head. 'Maureen didn't ruin my life. Our marriage was convenient, for both of us. There was never any question of—well, falling in love. She was older than I was, and I needed a housekeeper.'

'You still do,' put in Tamsyn humourlessly. 'Oh, Hywel, can't you see you're destroying me by refusing to see what's in front of your eyes? I came back—for you; only for you!'

Hywel brushed past her then, wrenching open the door to the street. 'We've got to go,' he insisted grimly. 'Your father's waiting.'

'Do you think he'll disapprove, is that what it is?' she cried, following him down the path.

Hywel turned to her then, his expression, in the shadowy light from a street lamp, ironic. 'I should think Lance has been left in little doubt as to my feelings for you after today,' he remarked heavily.

Tamsyn stared at him. 'What do you mean?'

'I think you know what I mean very well,' stated Hywel roughly. Then with a faint sigh of resignation he put his arm around her shoulders and pulled her close into its circle. 'All right, all right,' he breathed into her hair. 'I can't fight you any more. I want you too much to let you go again, may God forgive me.'

Tamsyn's face glowed. Wrapping her arms round his middle, she hugged herself against him. 'You mean it,' she said, with relief. 'Oh, Hywel, you won't regret it.'

Hywel opened the passenger door of the station wagon and put her firmly inside before walking round to slide in beside her. 'No, I don't think I will,' he agreed softly. 'But don't think it's going to be easy convincing your parents that it's the best thing for you.'

Tamsyn curled up close against him. 'So long as you want me, they can say what they like,' she replied, resting her head on his shoulder.

An hour later Tamsyn was seated comfortably on the couch in her father's living room, sipping a glass of brandy. Lance was seated beside her, while Hywel was standing before them, on the hearth.

Lance's face was beginning to lose the greyness that had been evident when they first arrived, but he was obviously finding it hard to act naturally. He had explained that Joanna and the baby were staying up at Nora's, as he had not expected to get home that night.

But although all the explanations had been made, and a call had been booked to Laura's house in Boston, Tamsyn sensed that her father had something else on his mind.

Finally Hywel said: 'What is it you want to ask me, Lance? Are you afraid that now your daughter's here, I'm going to take her away again?'

Tamsyn caught her breath, but her father merely stubbed out the cigarette he had been smoking with jerky movements, and nodded vigorously.

'Yes. Yes, you might as well know, Hywel. That's exactly what I've been thinking.'

Hywel tugged at the hair at the nape of his neck. 'I see.'

Tamsyn looked up at him swiftly and then back at her father's face. 'You know—about Hywel and me.' It was a statement.

Lance nodded again. 'Yes, I know. At least, I know the state Hywel was in when he thought you were dead.'

Tamsyn's eyes softened. 'Do you mind?'

Lance heaved a sigh. 'Of course I mind,' he muttered grimly. 'I'd be a fool to say otherwise. But that would apply whoever you were—well, in love with.'

'But you think I'm too old for her, don't you?' said Hywel dryly.

Lance studied his daughter's agonised expression for a few moments and then he shrugged. 'I don't know,' he answered. 'You are a lot older than she is, but...' He shook his head. 'I don't know. Tamsyn, how can you be sure about a thing like this?'

Tamsyn spread her hands helplessly. 'I just know,' she said. 'I've never felt this way about anyone before.'

'But you've scarcely had time——'

'Daddy, we've had five months! How much time do we need?'

'Even so.' Lance reached for another cigarette. 'Tamsyn, when I spoke to your mother on the telephone last night, she told me that you had mentioned this to her, and I had to accept that the main reason you came back here was for Hywel's sake.'

Tamsyn's eyes widened. 'She told you?'

'Of course.' Lance moved his shoulders impatiently. 'Tamsyn, last night we thought you were dead! We had to accept that we'd failed as parents and that Hywel meant more to you than either of us!'

'*Lance!*' Hywel's ejaculation was compassionate.

'Well, it's true, isn't it?' Lance sighed. 'Tamsyn, I'm not blaming you. That's the way it should be between a man and his wife. Hywel's a good man. There's no one I'd prefer in this role. It's just that—well, selfish as it may seem, I'd like you to myself for just a little bit longer.'

Tamsyn's brows drew together. 'But if I marry Hywel I shall be here—in the valley—for good!'

'I know that. At least, I know Hywel will always make his home here. But he travels sometimes, Tamsyn, and you would go with him. It can never be the same, after you're married, not really.'

Tamsyn cast a despairing look at Hywel, and his eyes narrowed. 'What would you like us to do, Lance?' he asked quietly.

Lance hesitated. 'I don't have the right——'

'I think you do,' Hywel was insistent.

'Very well then. Wait until Easter before you get married. Let Tamsyn stay here with us until then.'

Tamsyn twisted her hands together in her lap. She knew what Hywel's answer would be.

'Tamsyn?' he said, looking down at her. 'Will you do that?'

Tamsyn hesitated, looking first at Hywel, then at her father, then back to Hywel again, 'Oh, all right,' she nodded, pressing her lips together to stop them from trembling. 'Having waited five months, I suppose I can wait another three.'

She saw Hywel's expression relax. She knew he had been prepared for her to protest, to demand that he set aside her father's wishes and allow them to marry straight away.

But to demand those things would be to admit that there was some doubt attached to waiting, that in three months' time she might not be as sure of her feelings, whereas, in fact, she had been prepared to wait for ever if necessary.

Lance took a shaking breath. 'That's settled, then,' he said, and the telephone rang.

Laura was distraught, as was to be expected, and although no mention was made of Tamsyn returning to Boston, she insisted on stating that both she and Charles were flying over as soon as they could make arrangements to see her.

Tamsyn took it all very calmly in the circumstances. But now that everything was settled, now that her father had agreed to their marriage and would lend his support when her mother arrived, she felt an enveloping feeling of warmth and happiness. She looked up at Hywel and met his understanding gaze, and a faint smile lifted the corners of her mouth.

Six months later, Hywel and Tamsyn paid their first visit to Boston since their marriage. Laura had invited them for a few days' stopover on their way to New Zealand. Hywel was presently researching Maori history, and had been invited by an Auckland university to consult their libraries.

Three months of marriage had added a warm maturity to Tamsyn's natural good looks, and it was obvious from the way she looked at her husband that their relationship was satisfying in every way.

Hywel himself had put on weight and looked years younger, and Laura found it all a little hard to take, Tamsyn realised. Her mother had never experienced the kind of love she and Hywel shared, although she thought Charles genuinely cared for her.

Tamsyn herself was ecstatically happy. She had everything she had ever wished for, and she still found it hard to believe that only a year ago she had suffered the agonies of parting without hope of reconciliation.

Laura had given them the room that had been Tamsyn's until she left and Tamsyn smiled at her reflection in the dressing-table mirror as she sat brushing her hair before bed. It was strange, she thought, remembering the room and its associations, and sharing it with Hywel.

Laura had given a dinner party this evening, one of several she had arranged since their arrival, but Tamsyn was getting a little tired of having to share her husband with so many attractive women.

Glancing round now, she saw he was seated on the bed in his bathrobe, his hair damp from his shower, flicking through the pages of her photograph album. There were pictures of Tamsyn from the age of a few months up until the present, pictures of her receiving prizes at high school, playing tennis, in bathing suits; even pictures of the pets she had kept from time to time.

Rising from the stool, her hair a golden curtain of silk about her shoulders, she approached the bed and slid her arms round Hywel's neck from behind.

'Whatever are you looking at those old things for?' she asked teasingly, her hair brushing his face.

Hywel shook his head. 'I know your body and your mind,' he murmured huskily. 'But that's not enough. I want to know everything about you. Even what you were like as a baby.'

Tamsyn chuckled, resting her chin on the top of his head. 'Well, I weighed eight pounds at birth, and I used to kick off my covers, and I never would keep shoes on my feet——'

Hywel caught her wrist, drawing her round on to the bed beside him. 'All right, all right,' he said, throwing the album aside. 'Point taken.' He slid his hands up her arms inside the wide sleeves of the white lace negligée she was wearing. 'You're looking particularly beautiful this evening.'

Tamsyn smiled. 'I'm glad I please you.'

Hywel's expression became more disturbing. 'These few days in Boston have been enjoyable for you, haven't they?'

Tamsyn nodded. 'Reasonably so. Why? Haven't you enjoyed yourself?'

Hywel released her abruptly and rose to his feet. 'I've been wondering,' he said slowly, 'whether you'd prefer to stay on here for a couple of weeks while I go on to Auckland. I mean, I shall only be poking about in a lot of old relics——'

'Hywel!' Tamsyn stared at him in horror. 'Are you wanting to get rid of me?'

Hywel gave a muffled oath. 'Don't talk rubbish!' he muttered harshly.

Tamsyn rose unsteadily to her feet. 'Then what do you mean?'

Hywel turned to her, his clenched fists thrust into the pockets of his bathrobe. 'Tamsyn, I'm trying to be fair. You know your mother loves having you here——'

'Hywel, stop it! I won't listen to any more!' Tamsyn covered her ears with the palms of her hands. 'I don't want to stay here. I hate it here! Why, when I was brushing my hair I was wishing we could leave tomorrow!'

Hywel took a step forward. 'Do you mean that? You're not just saying it——'

'Oh, Hywel, don't you know me better than that by now?' she demanded tremulously, moving towards him.

Hywel hesitated only a moment longer and then he came forward, sweeping her up into his arms and depositing her on the bed before sliding on it beside her.

'Tamsyn,' he groaned urgently, burying his face in her scented neck, sliding the lace negligée from her shoulders. 'I adore you! And you don't know what agony it cost me to offer you the chance to stay on here.'

Tamsyn slid her bare arms round his neck, glorying in the hard strength of his body pressing hers down into the softness of the mattress. This was where she belonged, with Hywel, and she had known that a lot longer than he...

Mills & Boon Classics

The very best of Mills & Boon
romances, brought back for those of
you who missed reading them
when they were first published.

There are three other Classics for you to collect this
May

A MAN APART
by Jane Donnelly

Everyone who knew Libby Mason hoped that she and Ian
Blaney would make a match of it, and they were all quick to
point out how misguided she would be to entertain any
romantic ideas about the 'outsider' Adam Roscoe. But wasn't
it just possible that 'everyone' might be wrong?

RAPTURE OF THE DESERT
by Violet Winspear

Chrys didn't trust men, and Anton de Casenove was just the
type of man she most needed to be on her guard against —
half Russian prince, half man of the desert; a romantic com-
bination. Could even Chrys be proof against it?

THE CRESCENT MOON
by Elizabeth Hunter

When Madeleine was stranded in Istanbul, there was no one
to whom she could turn for help except the lordly Maruk Bey,
who had told her that he found her 'dark, mysterious, and
very, very beautiful.' Could Madeleine trust such a man to
aid her?